A book is like a world you can carry around with you.

Dedicated to Matilda, who taught me
how to draw like Henrietta;
to Clementina, whose stuffed bunny
is named "My Favorite"; and to Emma,
who always looks great in my hats.

LINIERS—

Editorial Director: FRANÇOISE MOULY

Book Design: FRANÇOISE MOULY & MAGDALENA OKECKI

RICARDO LINIERS' artwork was drawn in ink, watercolor, and colored pencils.

A TOON Book™ © 2015 Liniers & TOON Books, an imprint of RAW Junior, LLC, 27 Greene Street, New York, NY 10013. No part of this book may be used or reproduced in any manner whatsoever without written permission except in the case of brief quotations embodied in critical articles and reviews. TOON Graphics™, TOON Books®, LITTLE LIT® and TOON Into Reading!™ are trademarks of RAW Junior, LLC. All rights reserved. All our books are Smyth Sewn (the highest library-quality binding available) and printed with soy-based inks on acid-free, woodfree paper harvested from responsible sources. Printed in China by C&C Offset Printing Co., Ltd. Distributed to the trade by Consortium Book Sales and Distribution, Inc.; orders (800) 283-3572 34; orderentry@perseusbooks.com; www.cbsd.com. Library of Congress Cataloging-in-Publication Data available upon request. LCNN: 2015004010
A Spanish edition, *Escrito y Dibujado por Enriqueta* (ISBN: 978-1-935179-91-7), is also available.

ISBN 978-1-935179-90-0 (English language hardcover)
16 17 18 19 20 21 C&C 10 9 8 7 6 5 4 3

WRITTEN AND DRAWN BY HENRIETTA

A TOON BOOK BY
LINIERS

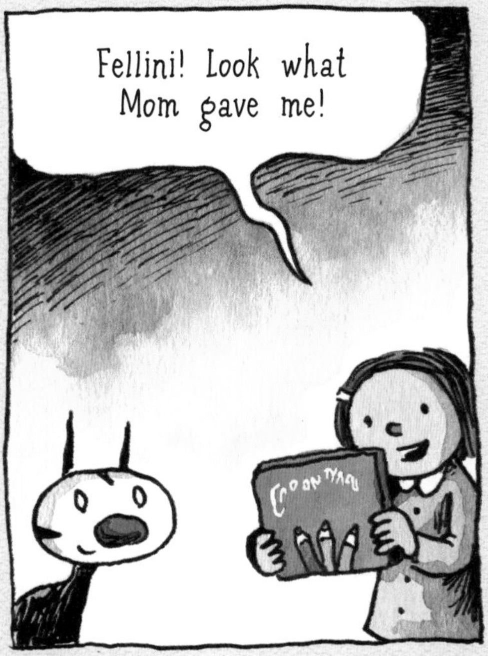
Fellini! Look what Mom gave me!

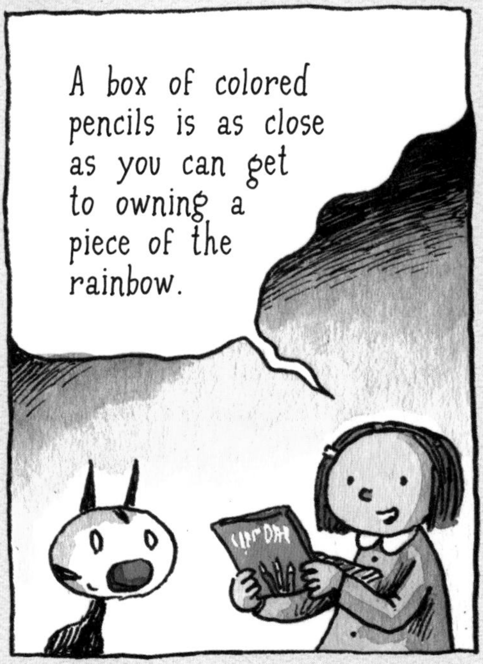
A box of colored pencils is as close as you can get to owning a piece of the rainbow.

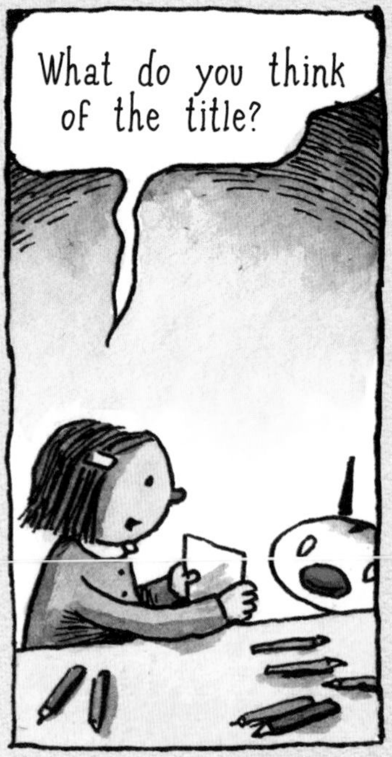
What do you think of the title?

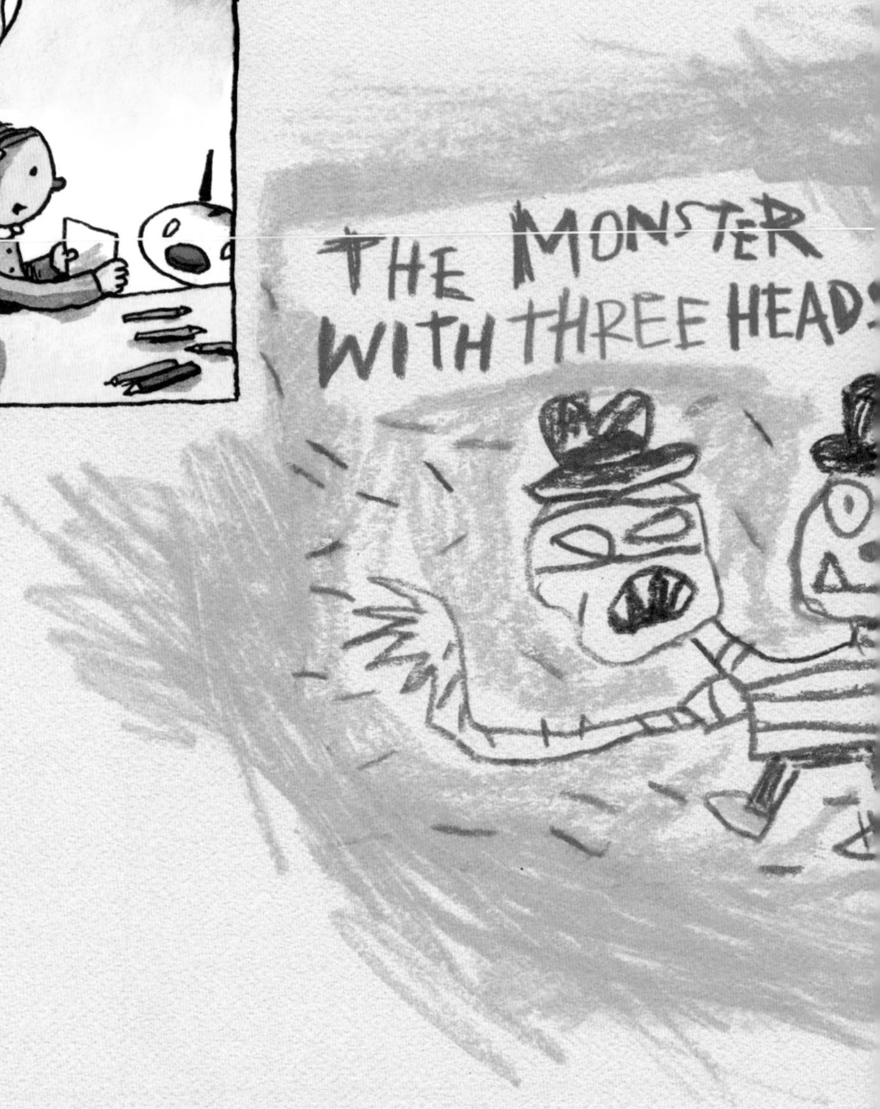
THE MONSTER
WITH THREE HEAD

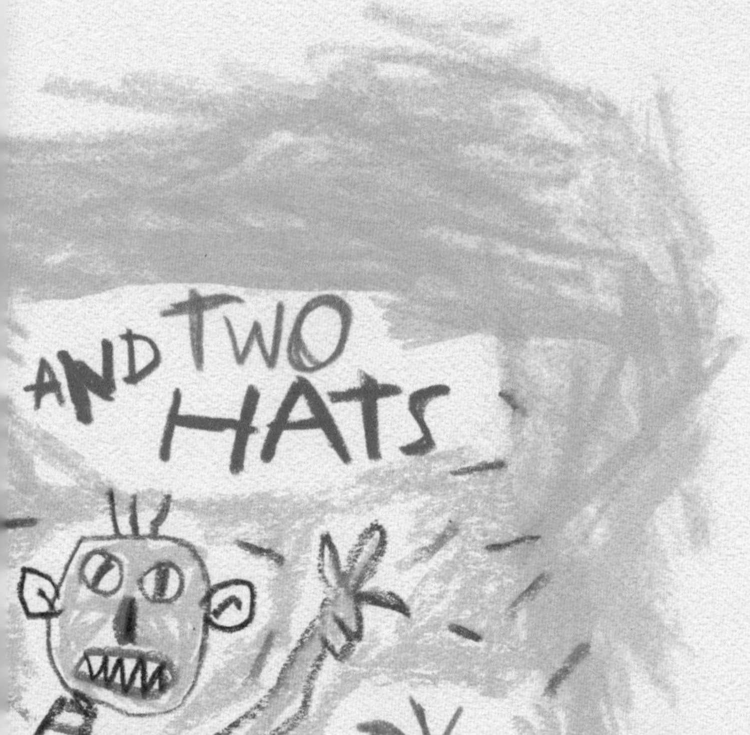
AND TWO
HATS
BY
HENRIETTA

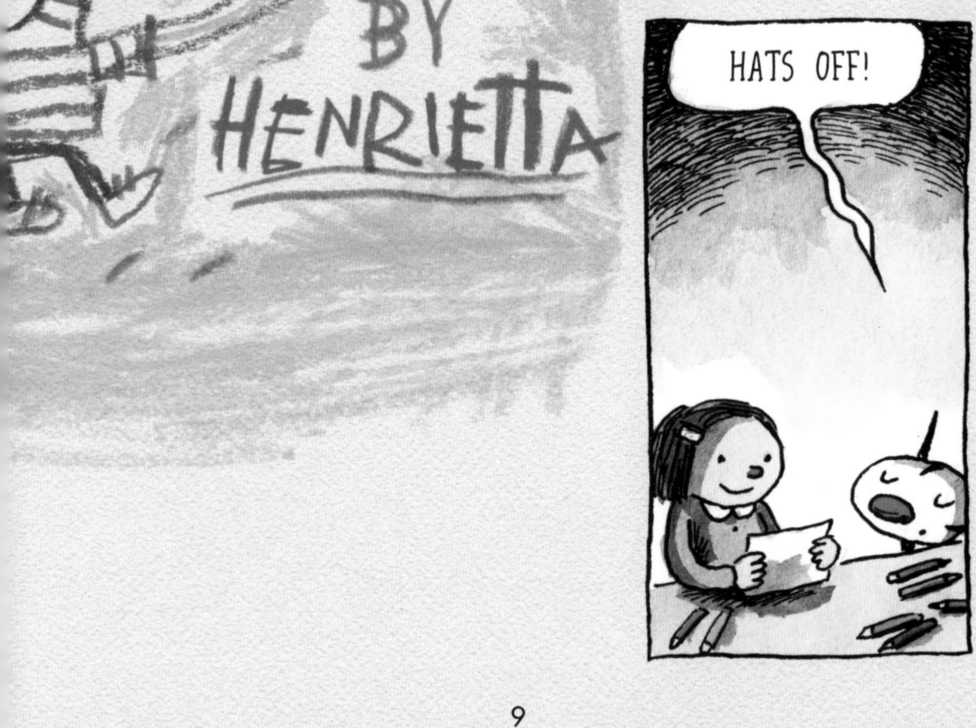
HATS OFF!

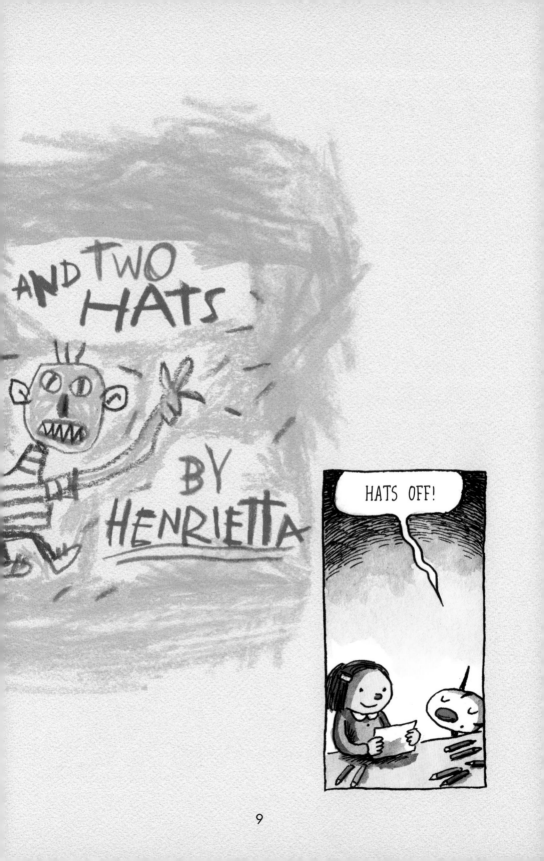

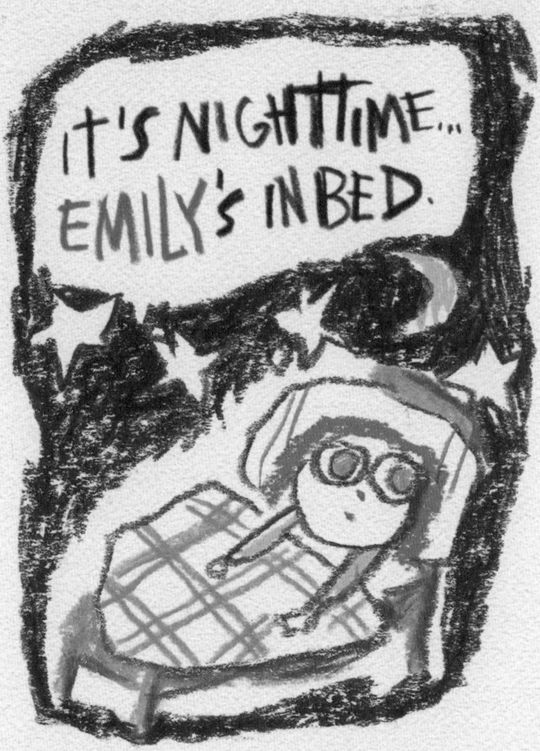
IT'S NIGHTTIME...
EMILY'S IN BED.

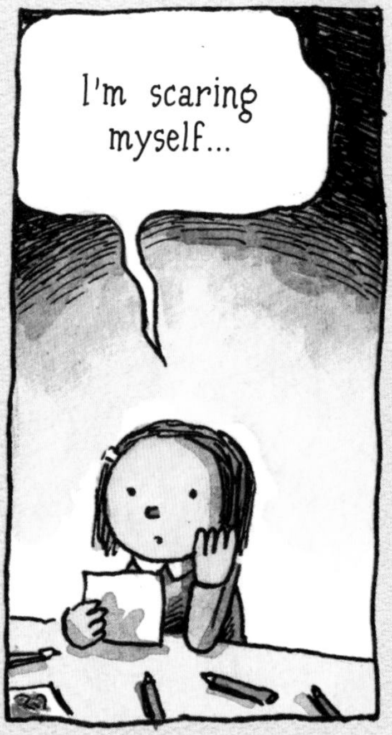
I'm scaring myself...

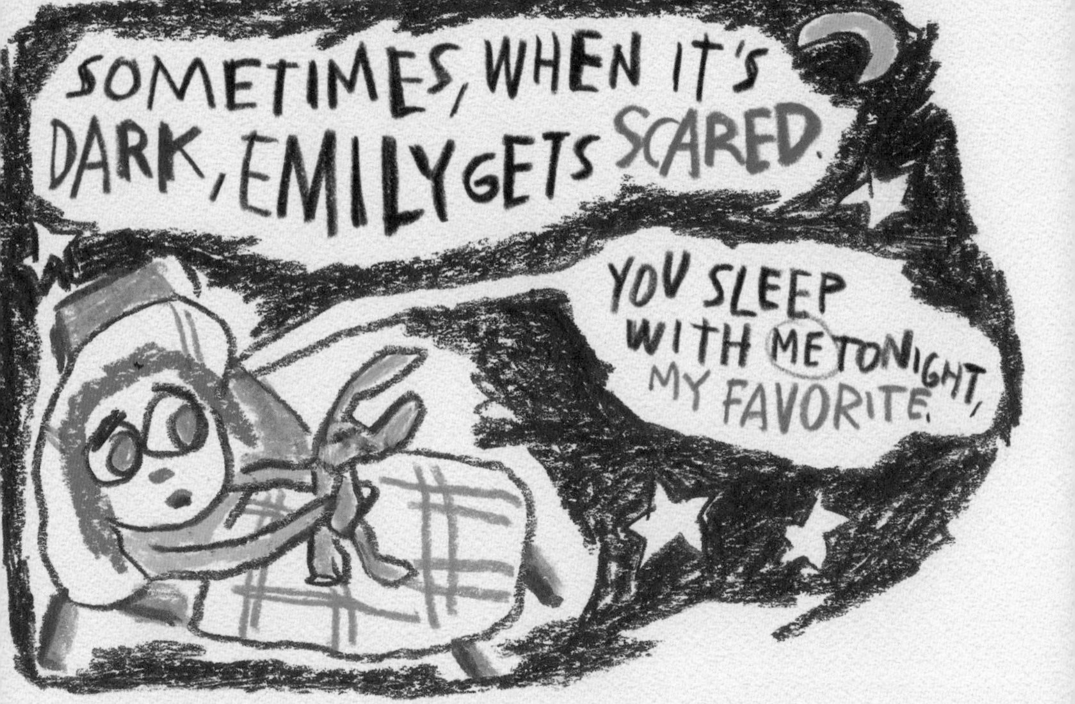
SOMETIMES, WHEN IT'S DARK, EMILY GETS SCARED.
YOU SLEEP WITH ME TONIGHT, MY FAVORITE.

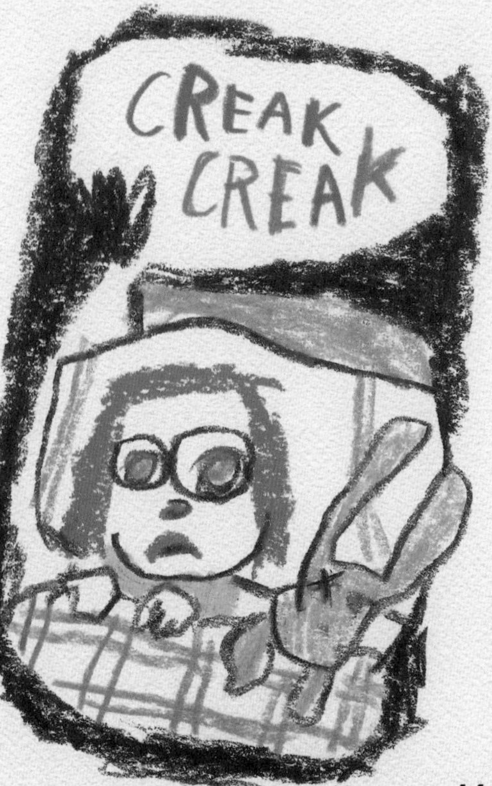
CREAK CREAK

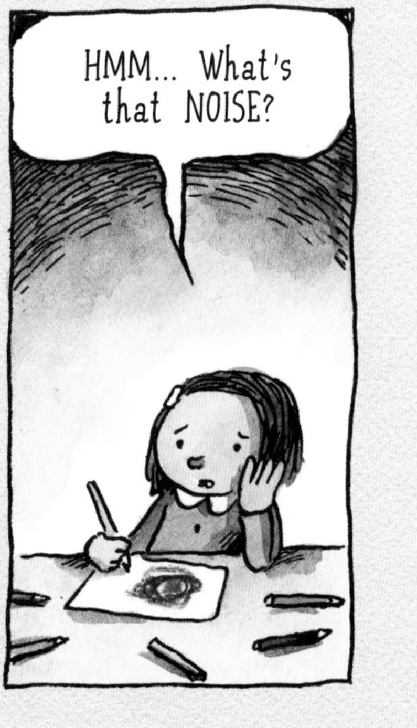
HMM... What's that NOISE?

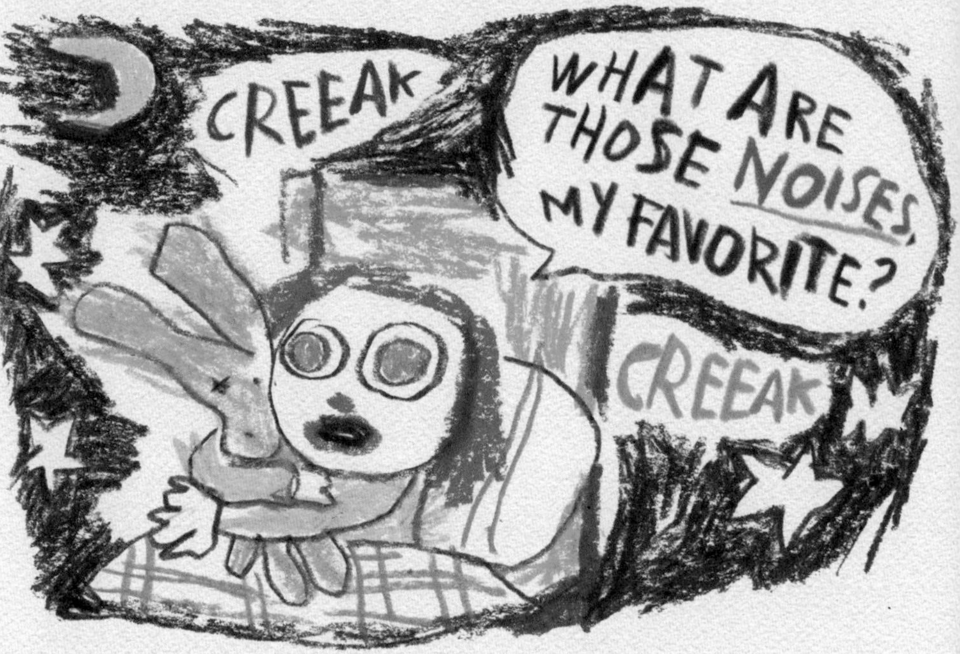
CREEAK
WHAT ARE THOSE NOISES, MY FAVORITE?
CREEAK

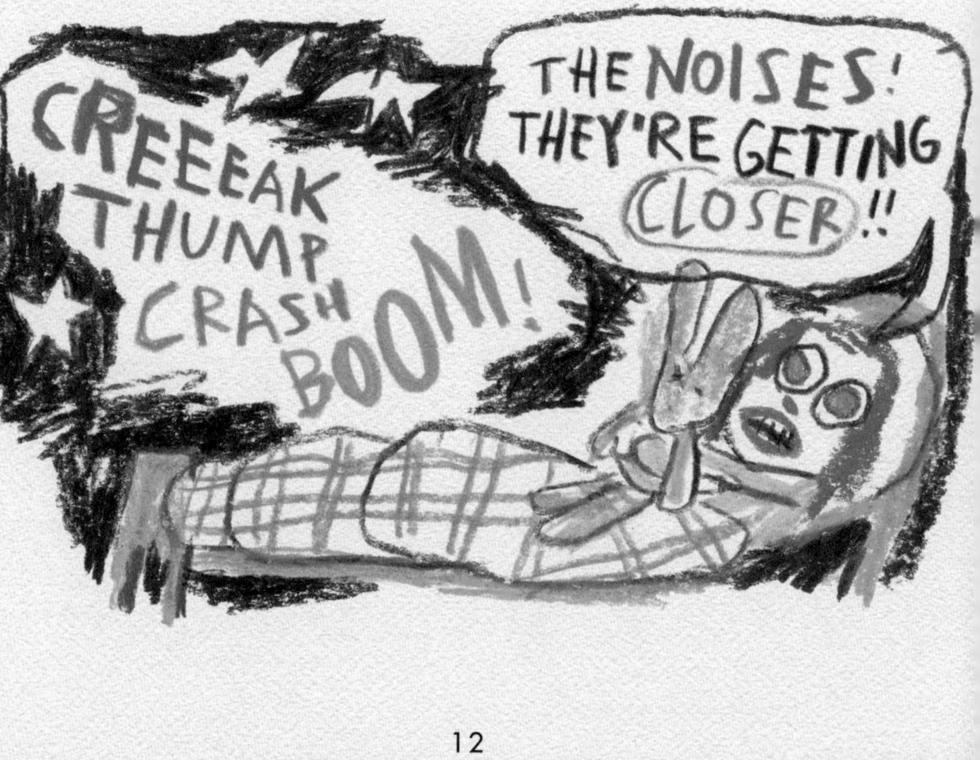
CREEEAK THUMP CRASH BOOM!
THE NOISES! THEY'RE GETTING CLOSER!!

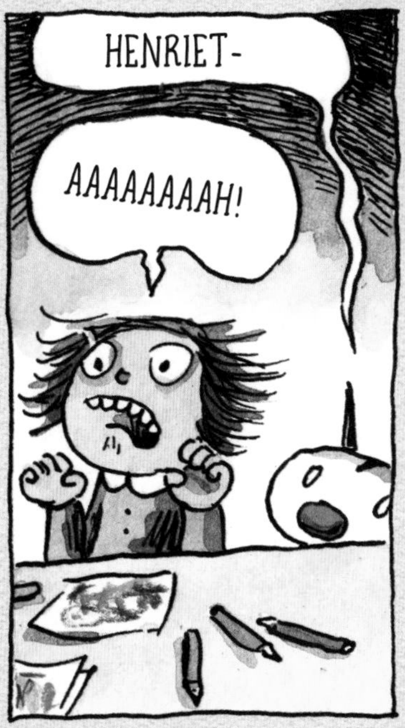
HENRIET-
AAAAAAAAH!

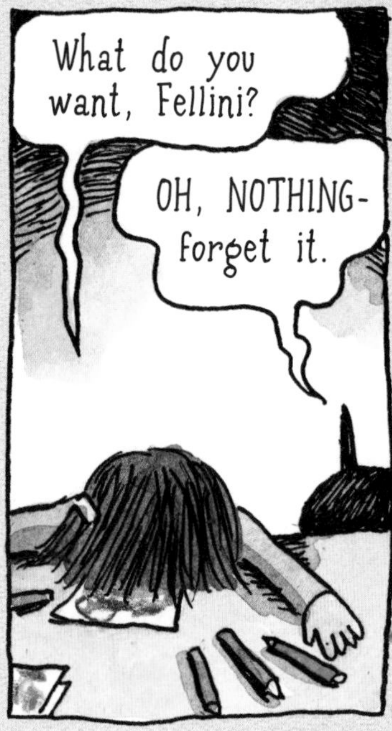
What do you want, Fellini?
OH, NOTHING- forget it.

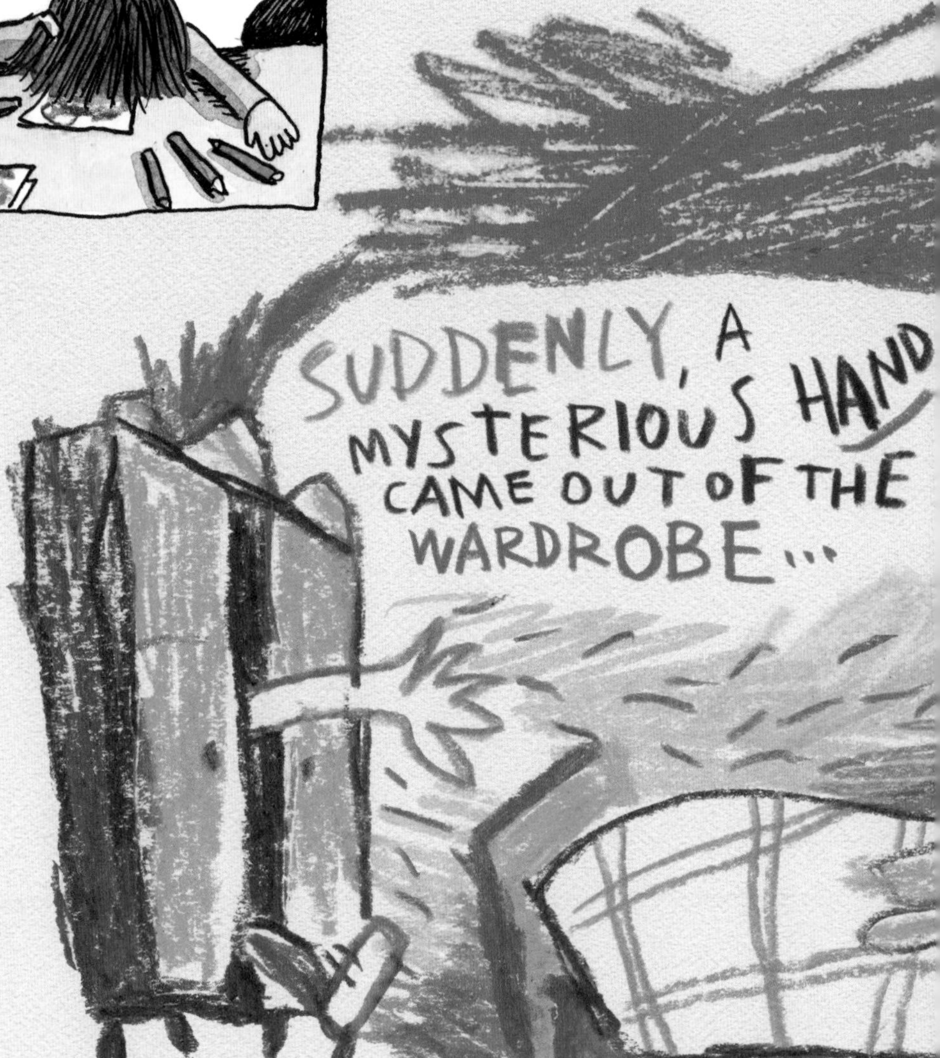
SUDDENLY, A MYSTERIOUS HAND CAME OUT OF THE WARDROBE...

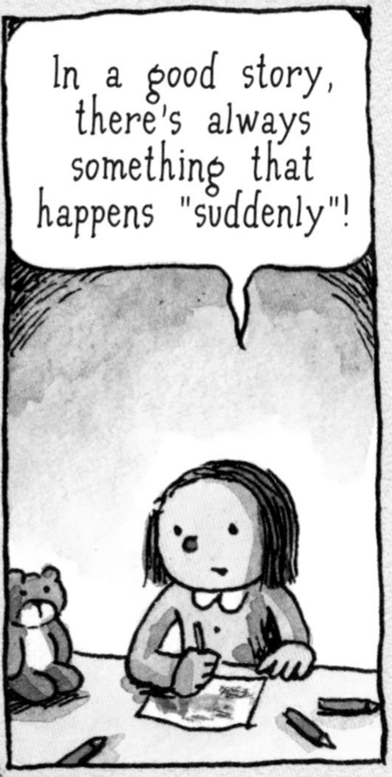
In a good story, there's always something that happens "suddenly"!

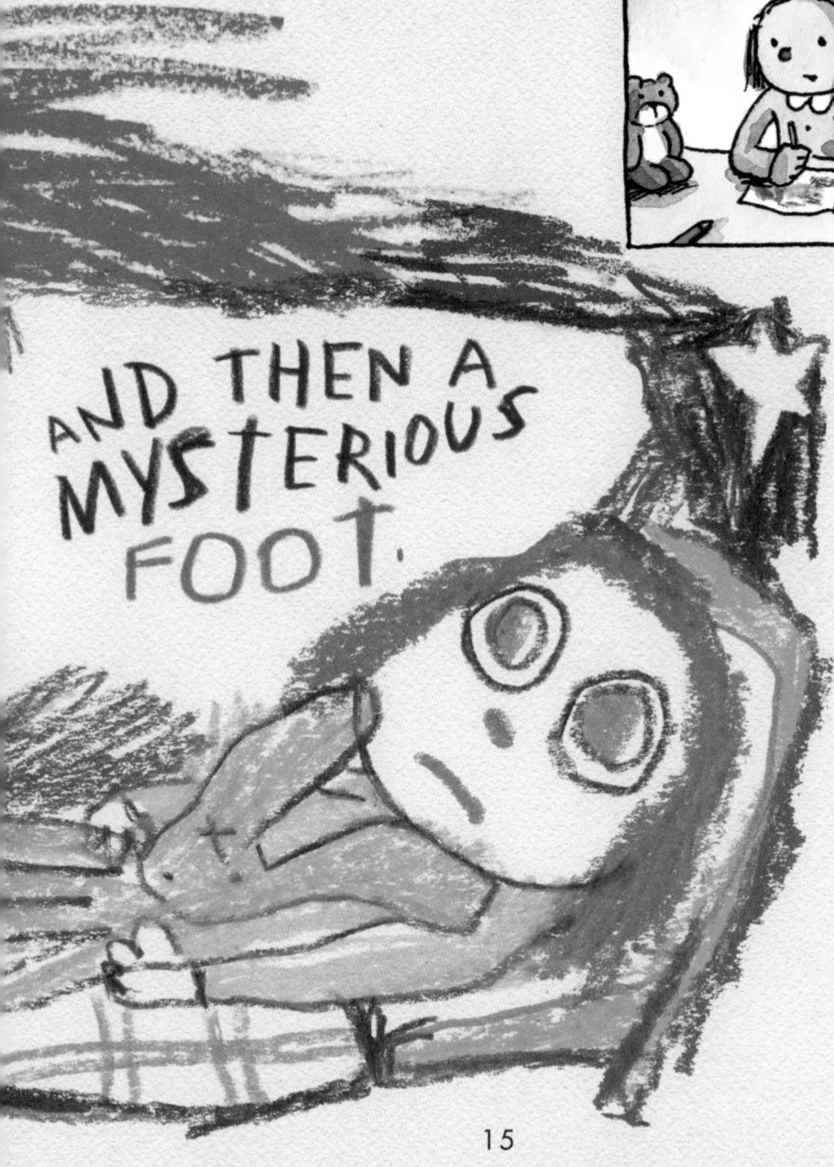
AND THEN A MYSTERIOUS FOOT.

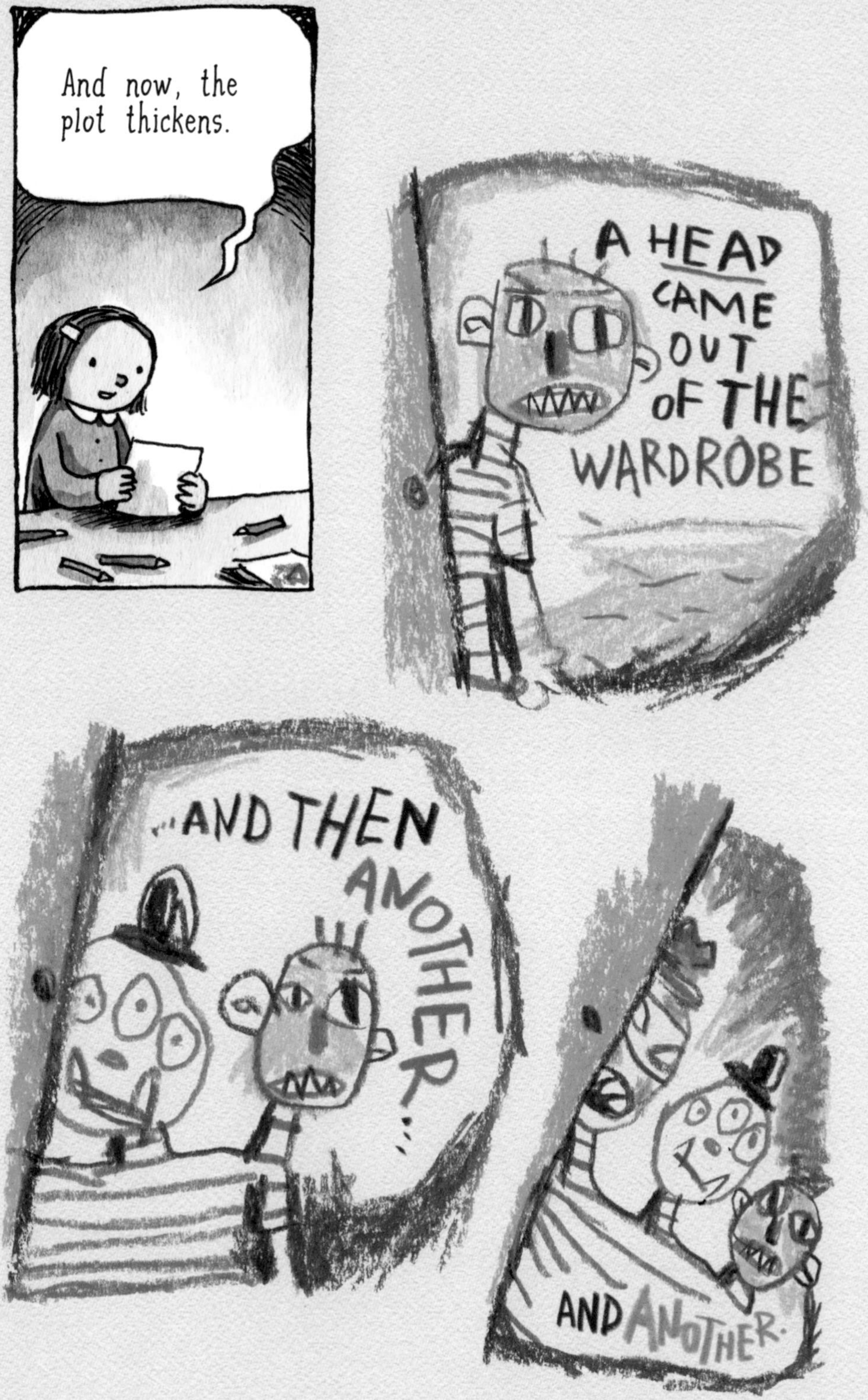

And now, the plot thickens.
A HEAD CAME OUT OF THE WARDROBE
...AND THEN ANOTHER...
AND ANOTHER.

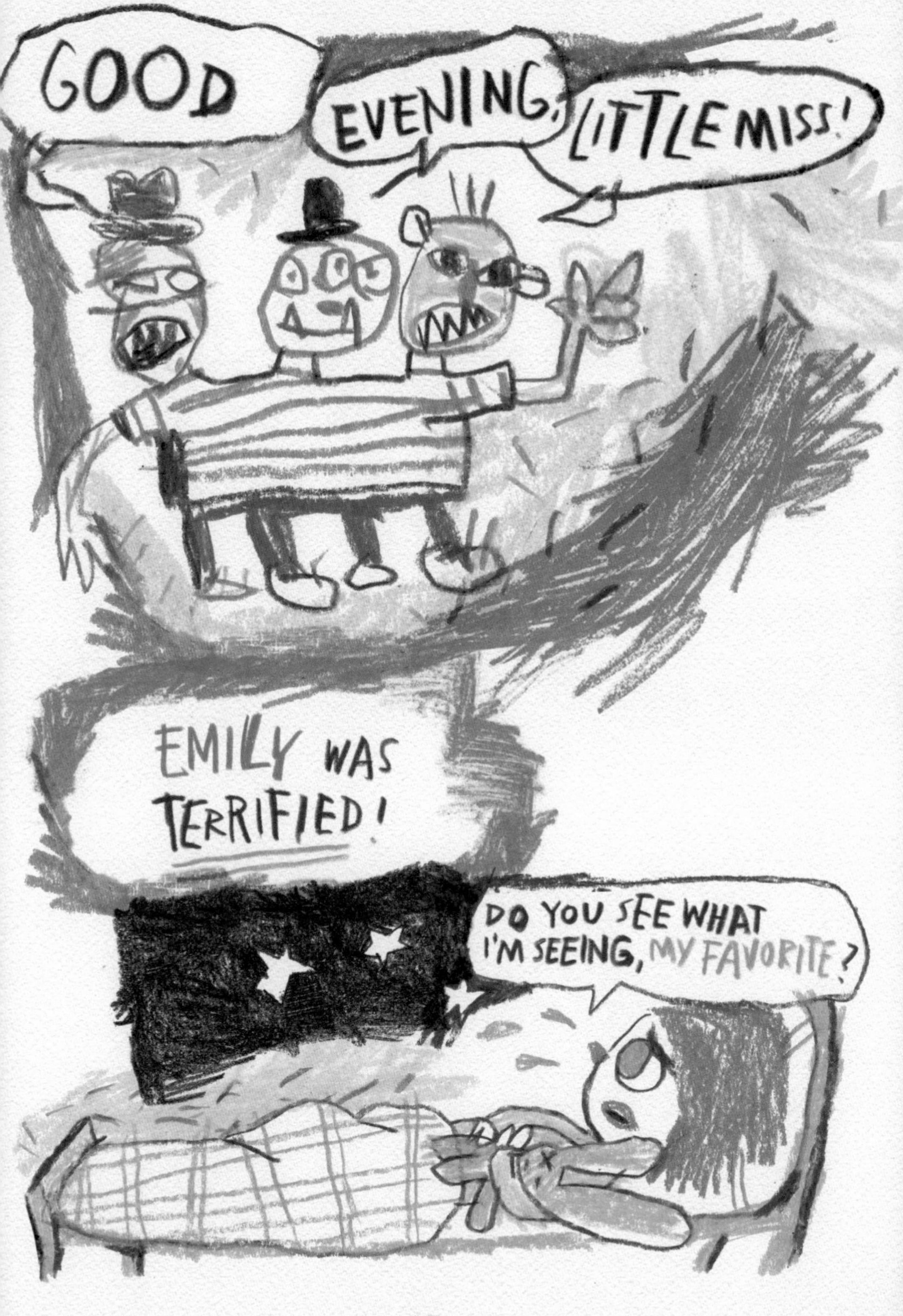
GOOD
EVENING,
LITTLE MISS!
EMILY WAS TERRIFIED!
DO YOU SEE WHAT I'M SEEING, MY FAVORITE?

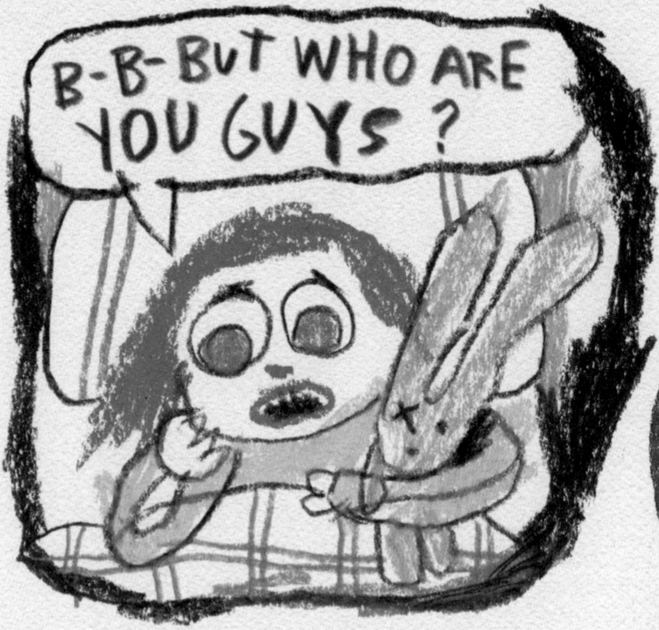
B-B-BUT WHO ARE YOU GUYS?

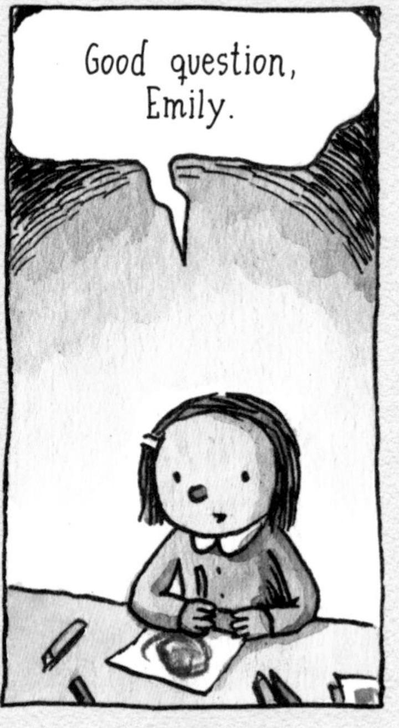
Good question, Emily.

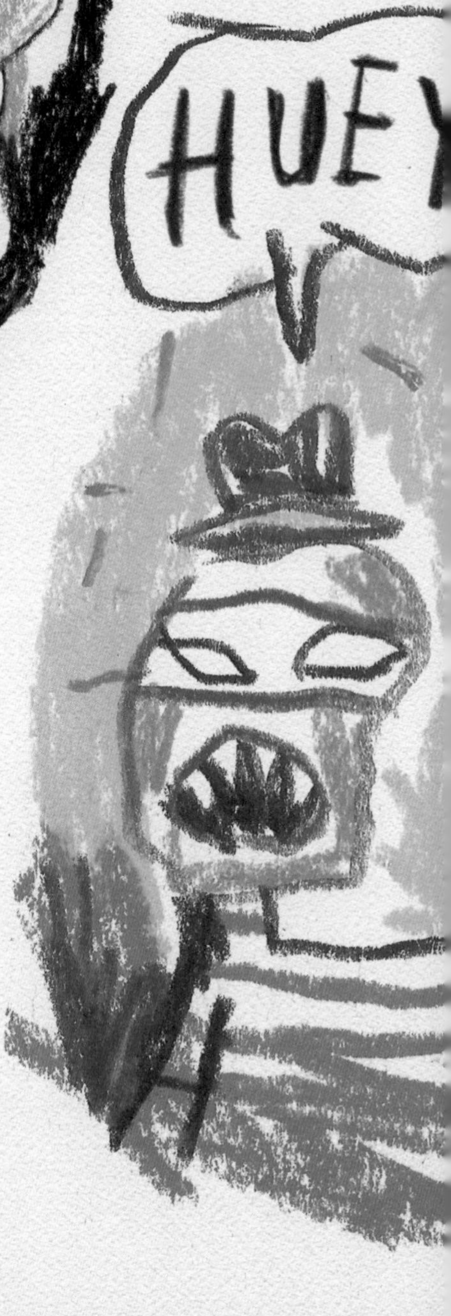
HUEY

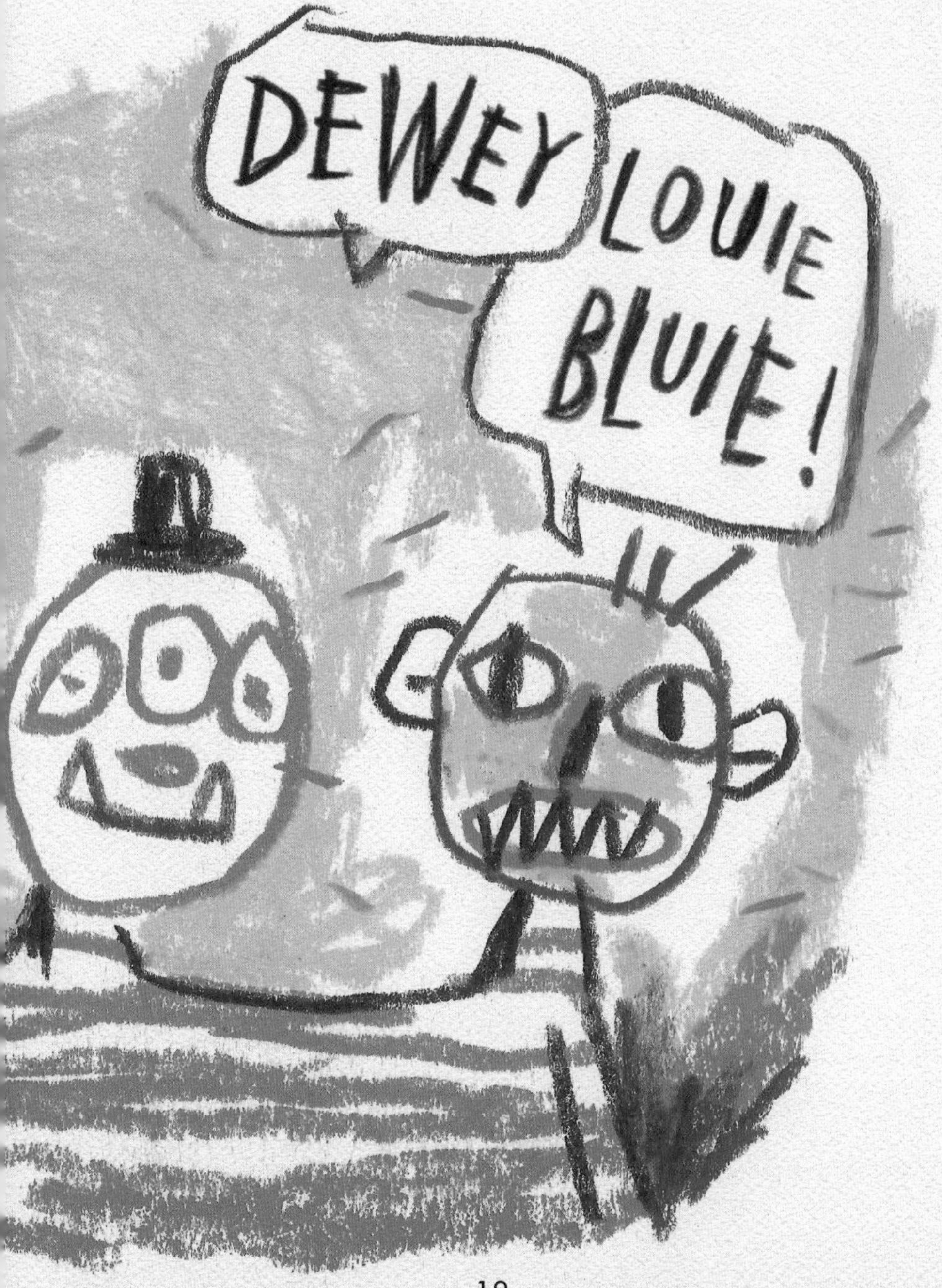
DEWEY
LOUIE BLUIE!

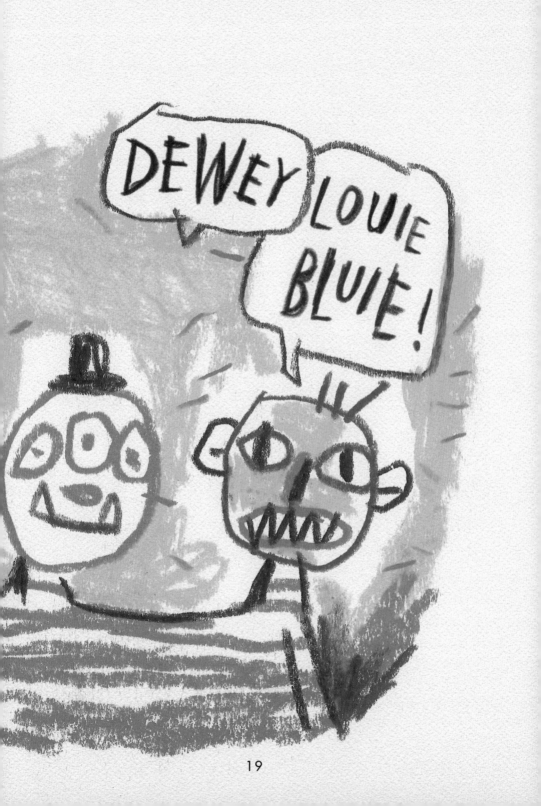

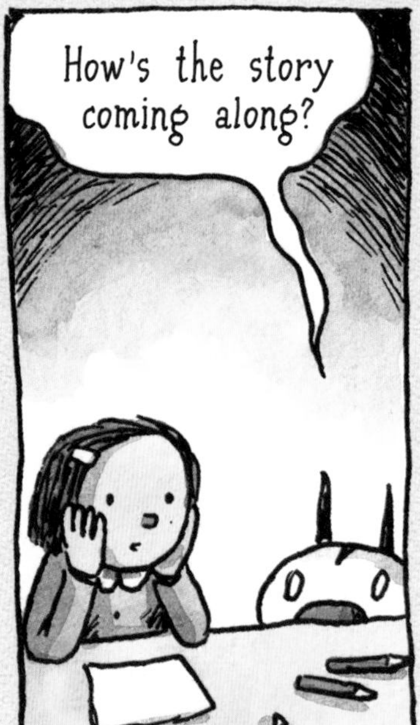
How's the story coming along?

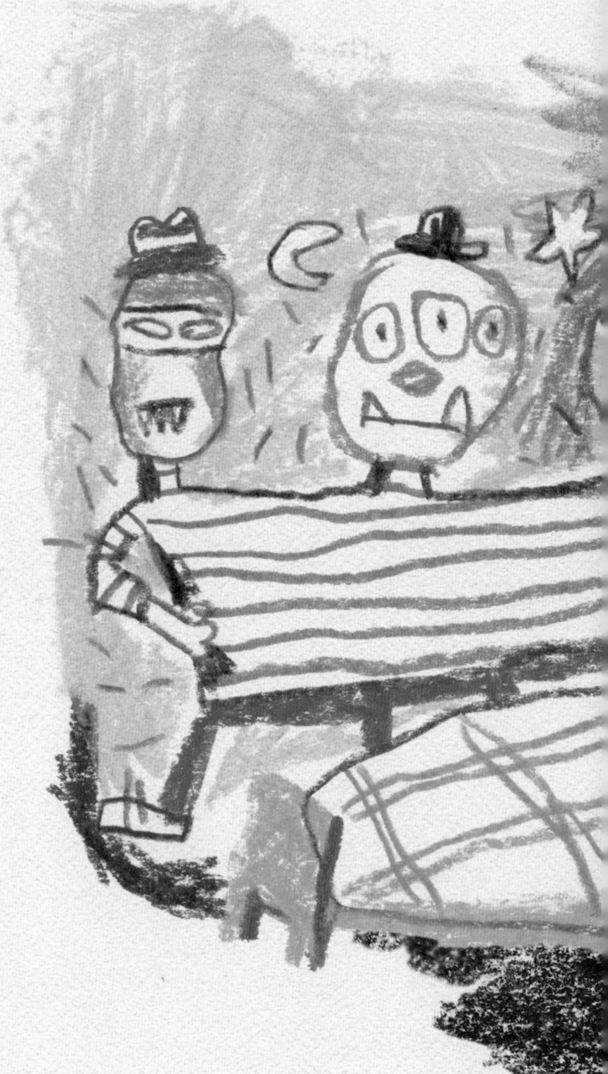

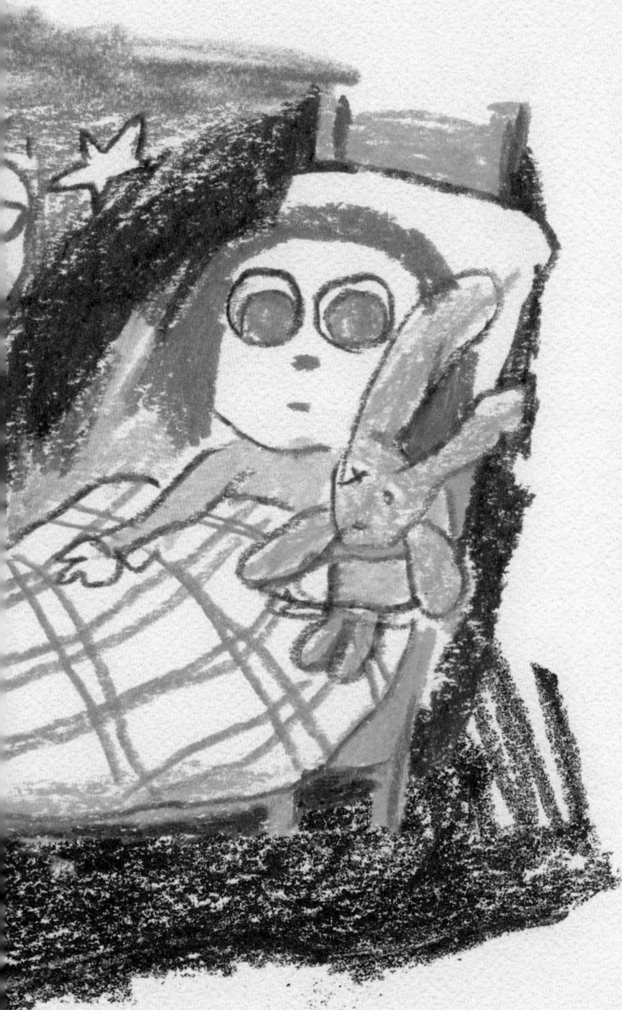

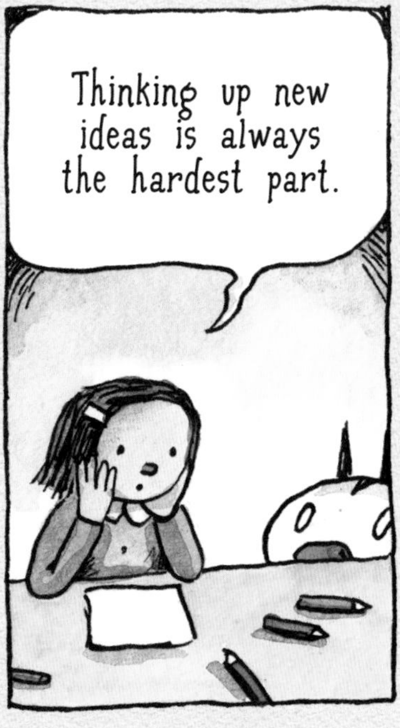
Thinking up new ideas is always the hardest part.

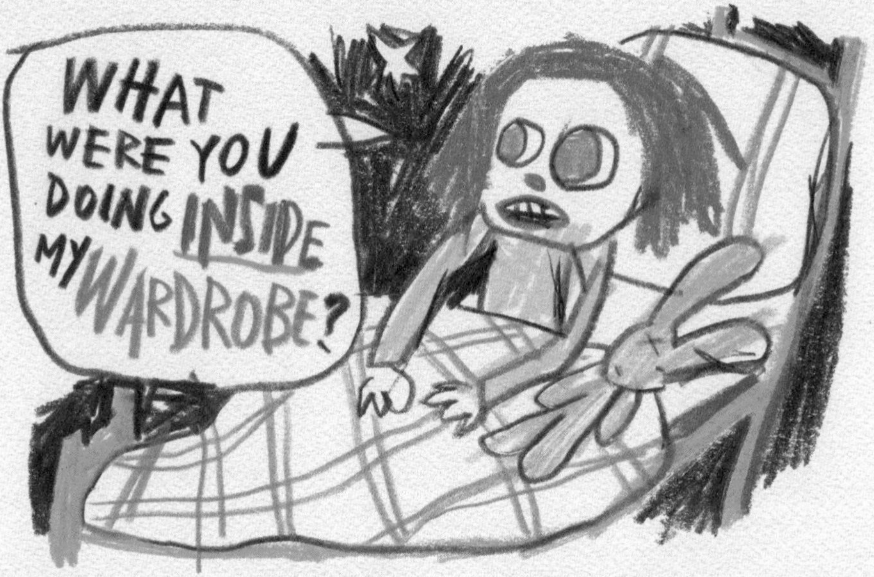
WHAT WERE YOU DOING INSIDE MY WARDROBE?

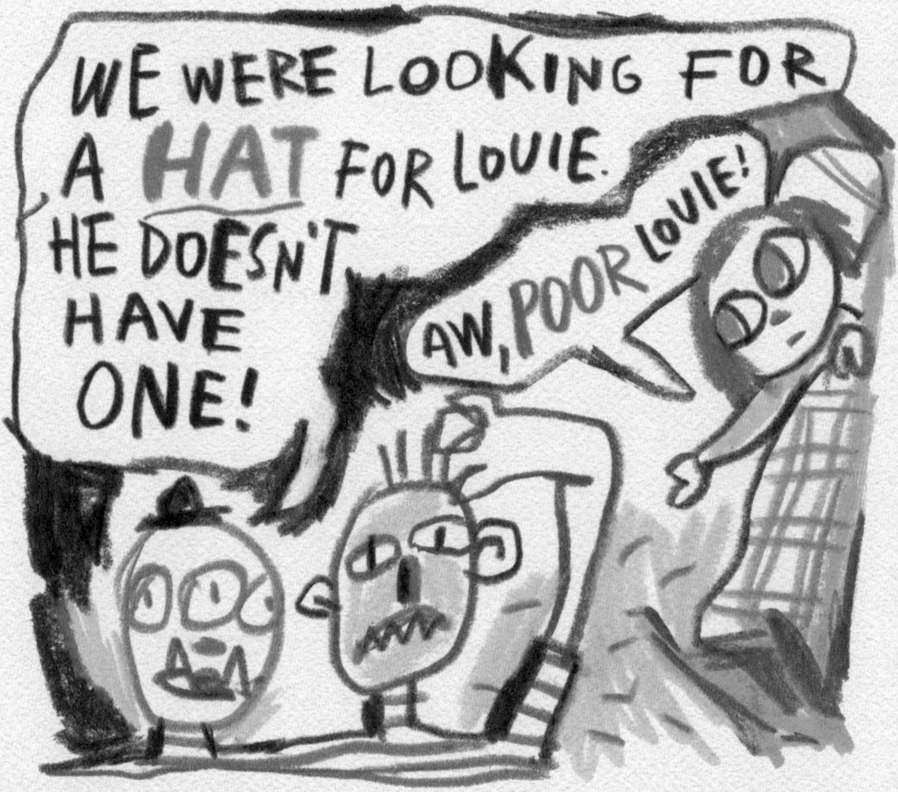
WE WERE LOOKING FOR A HAT FOR LOUIE. HE DOESN'T HAVE ONE!
AW, POOR LOUIE!

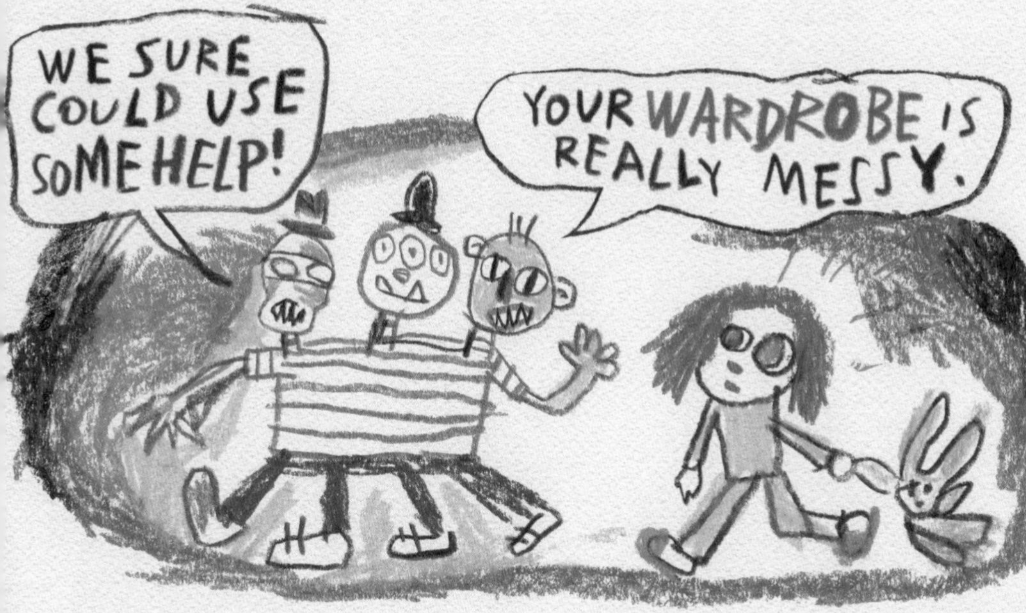
WE SURE COULD USE SOME HELP!
YOUR WARDROBE IS REALLY MESSY.

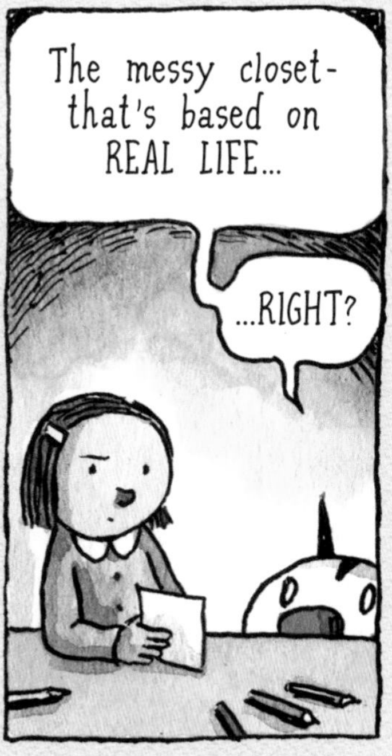
The messy closet-that's based on REAL LIFE...
...RIGHT?

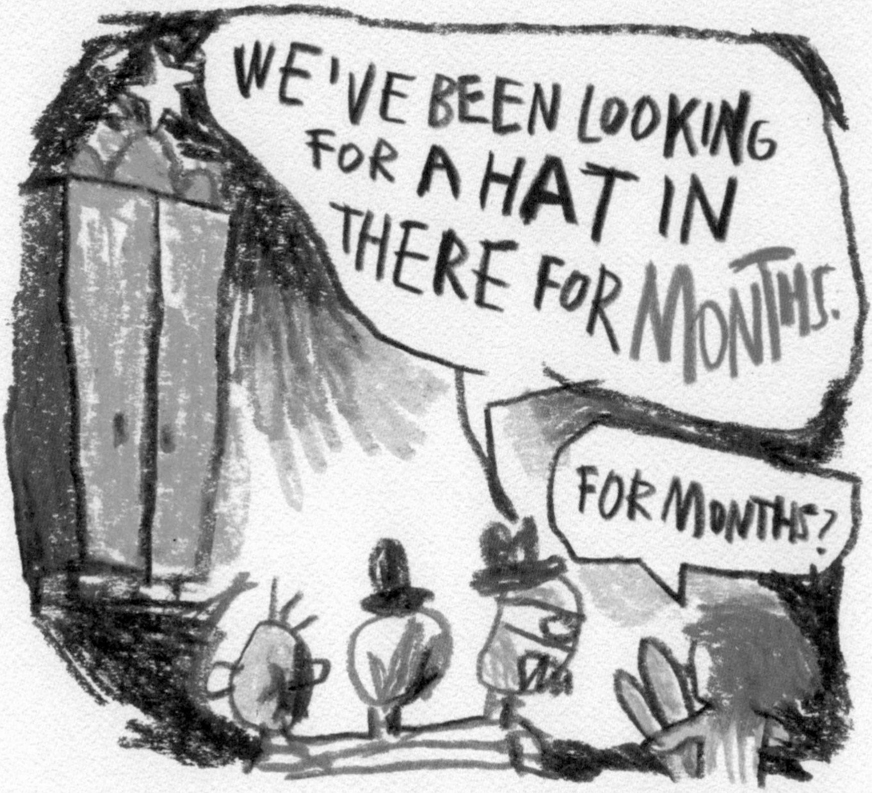
WE'VE BEEN LOOKING FOR A HAT IN THERE FOR MONTHS.
FOR MONTHS?
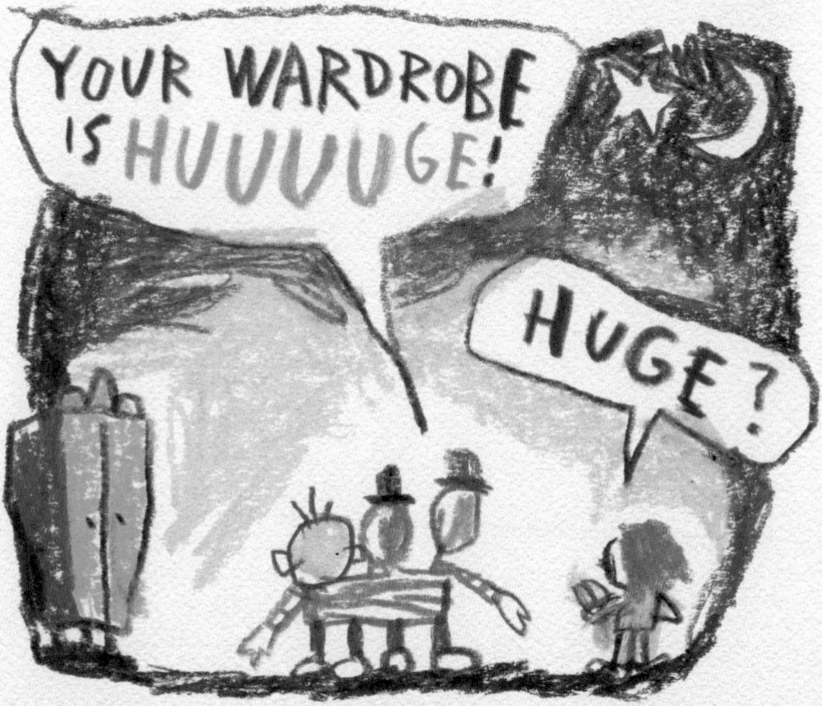
YOUR WARDROBE IS HUUUUGE!
HUGE?

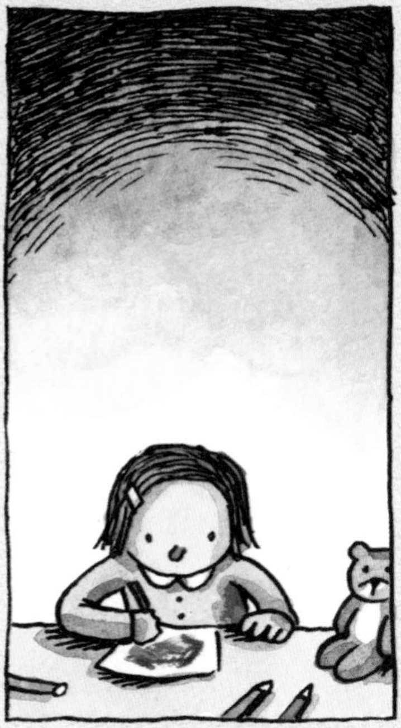

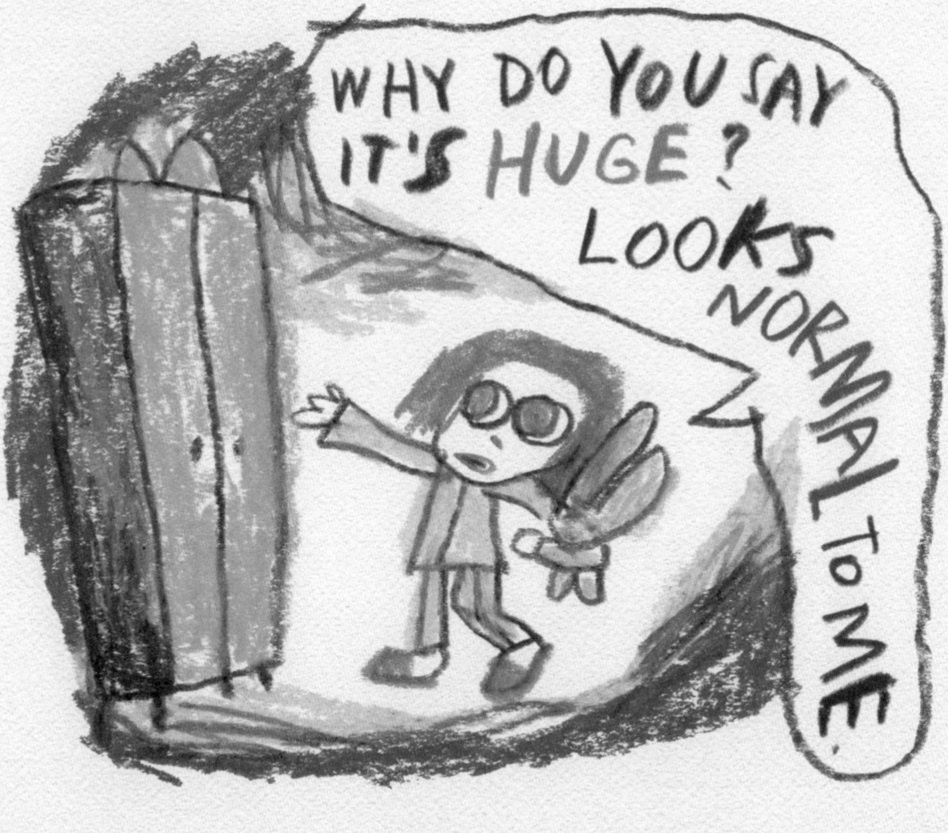
WHY DO YOU SAY IT'S HUGE? LOOKS NORMAL TO ME.

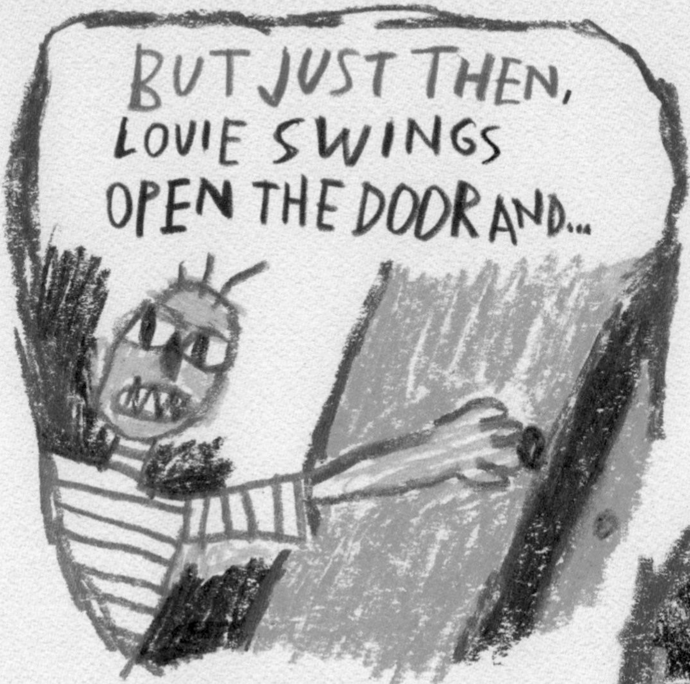
BUT JUST THEN,
LOUIE SWINGS
OPEN THE DOOR AND...

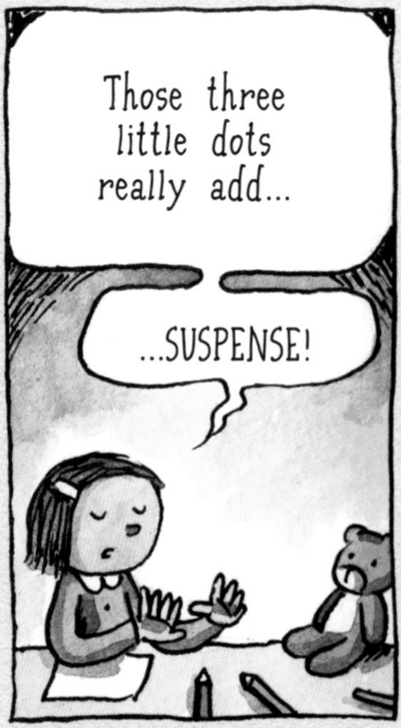
Those three little dots really add...
...SUSPENSE!

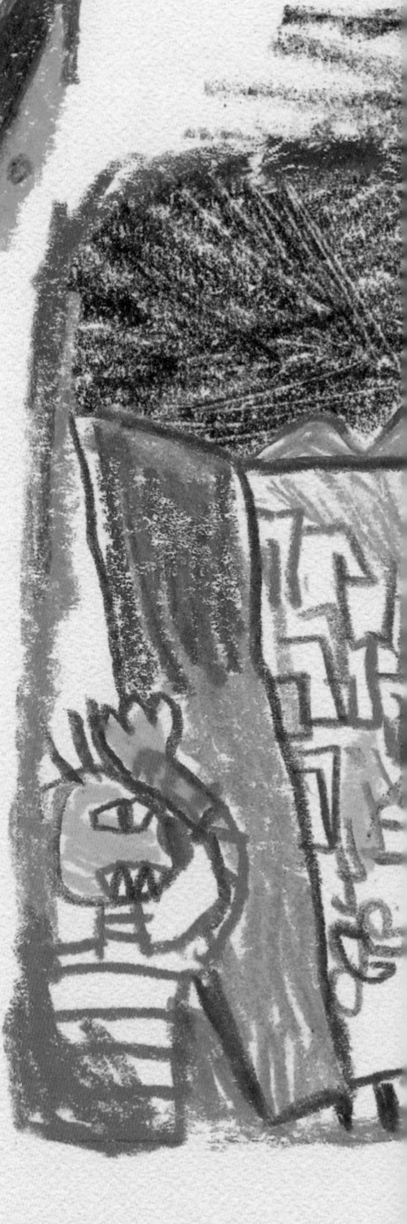

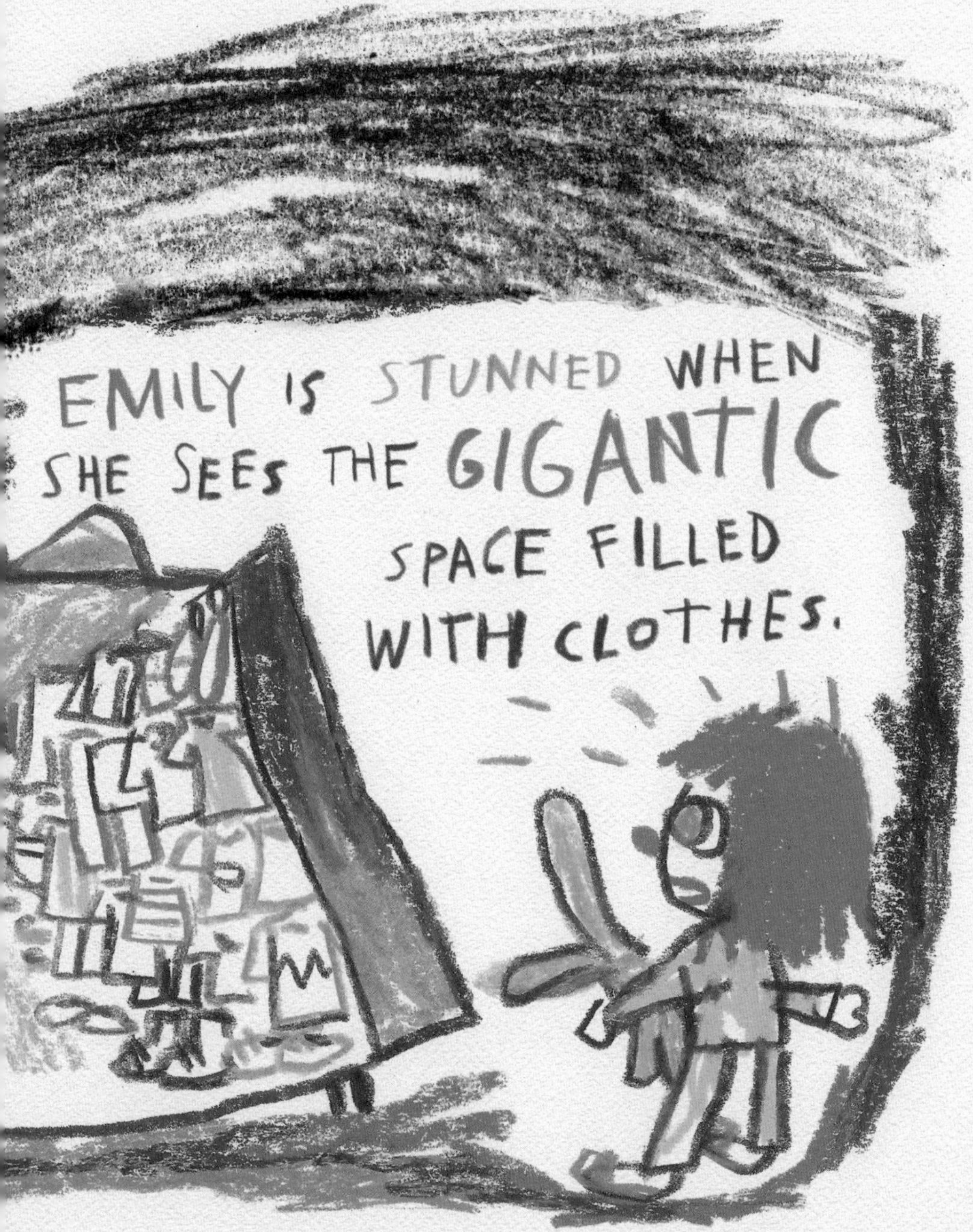
EMILY IS STUNNED WHEN
SHE SEES THE GIGANTIC
SPACE FILLED
WITH CLOTHES.

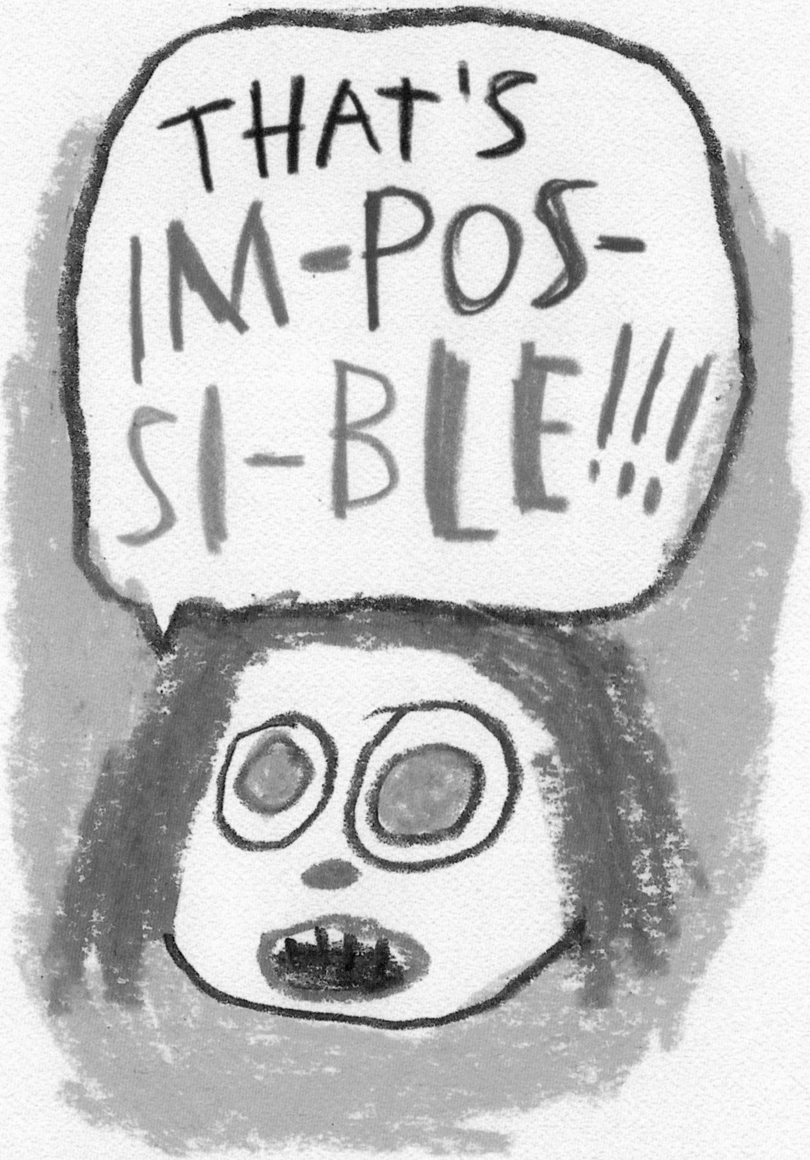
THAT'S
IM-POS-
SI-BLE!!!

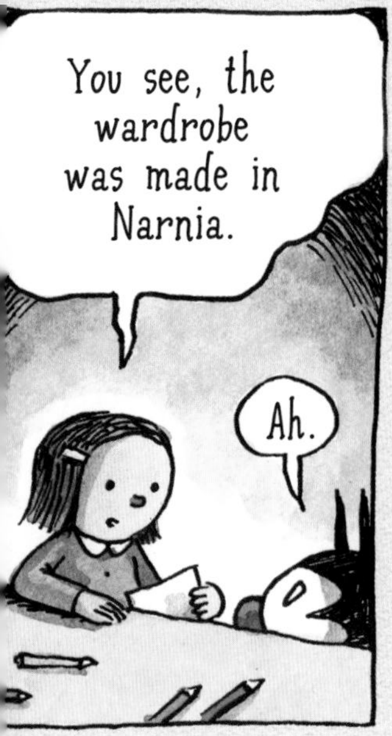
You see, the wardrobe was made in Narnia.
Ah.

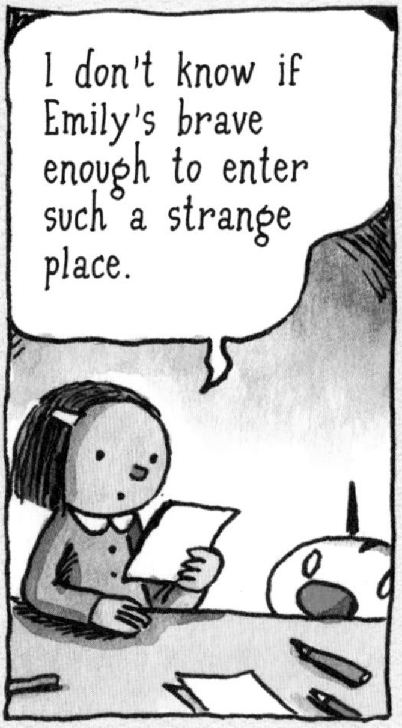
I don't know if Emily's brave enough to enter such a strange place.

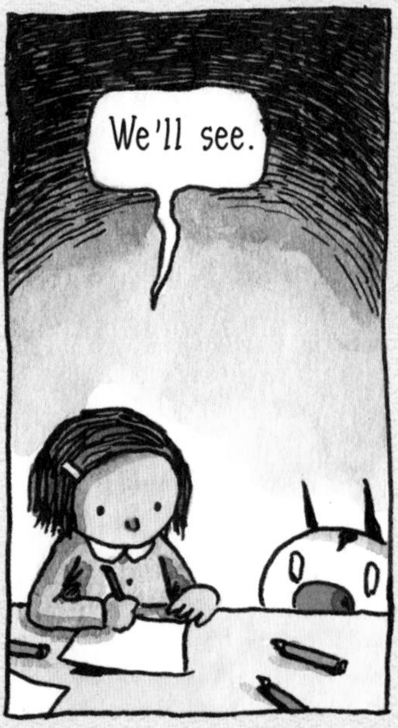
We'll see.

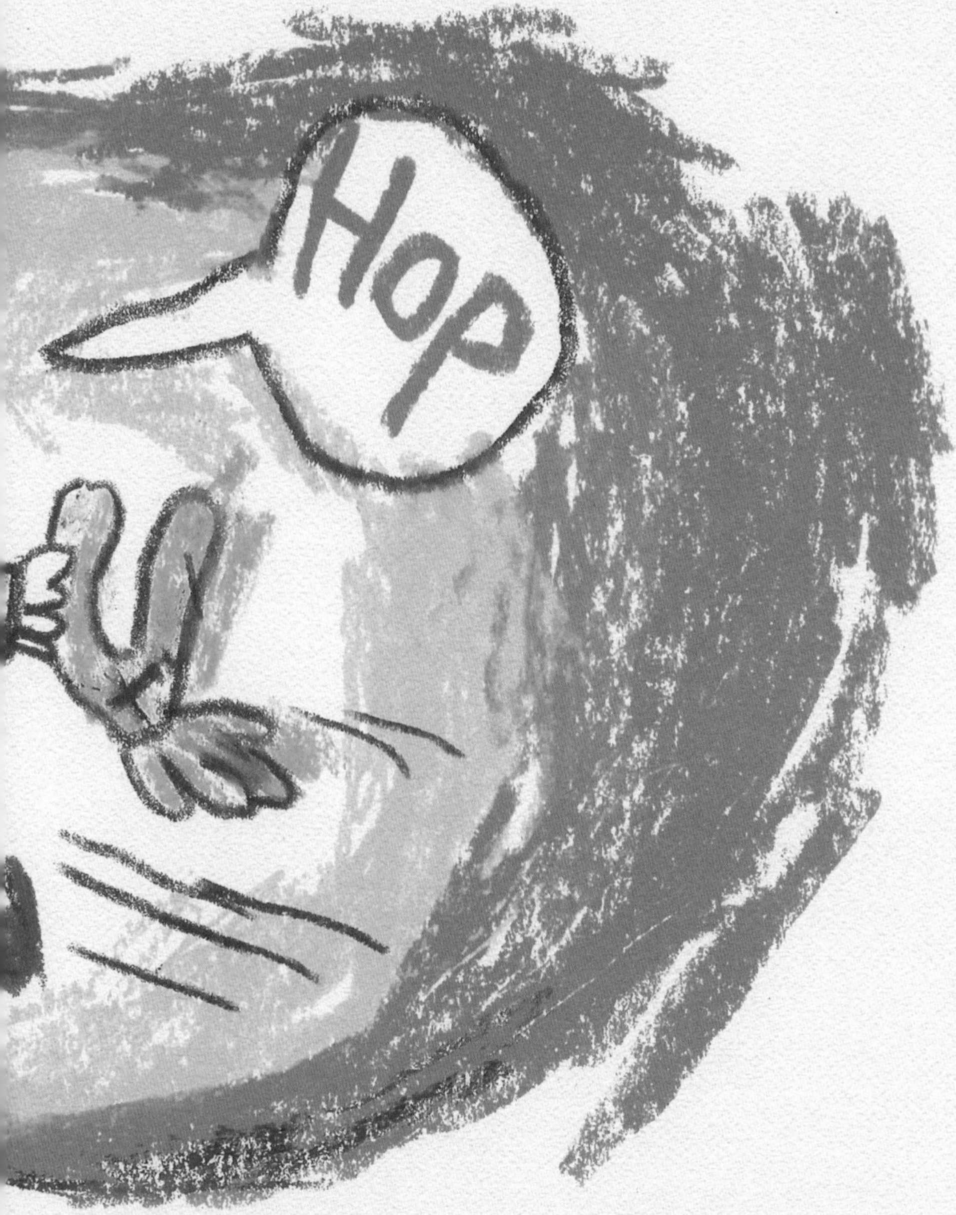
Hop

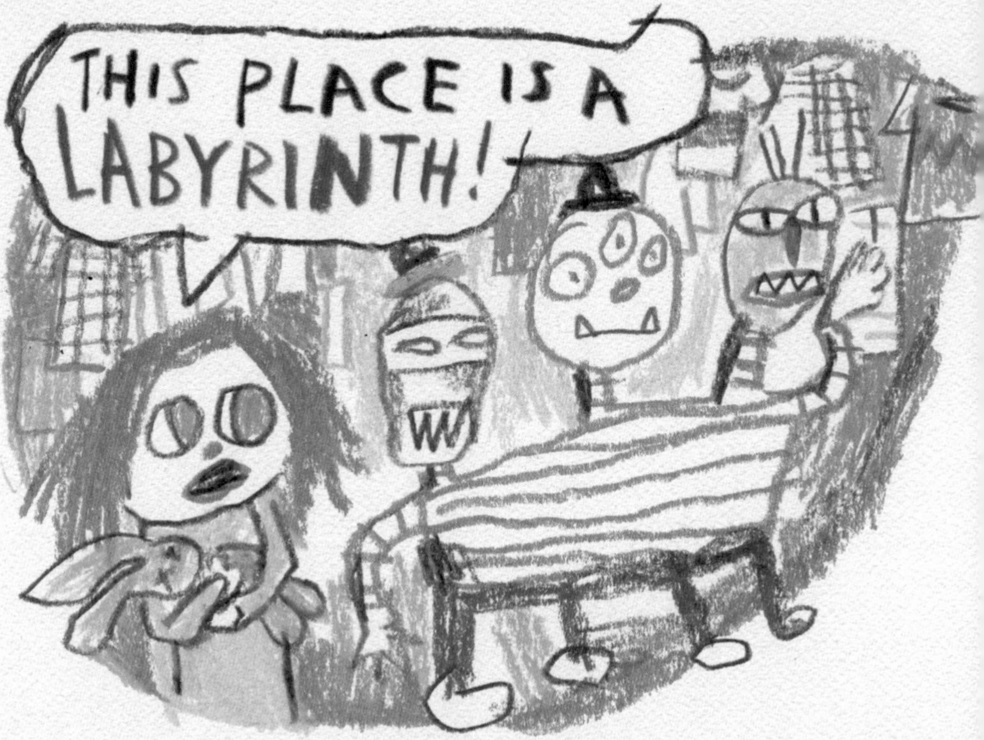
THIS PLACE IS A LABYRINTH!

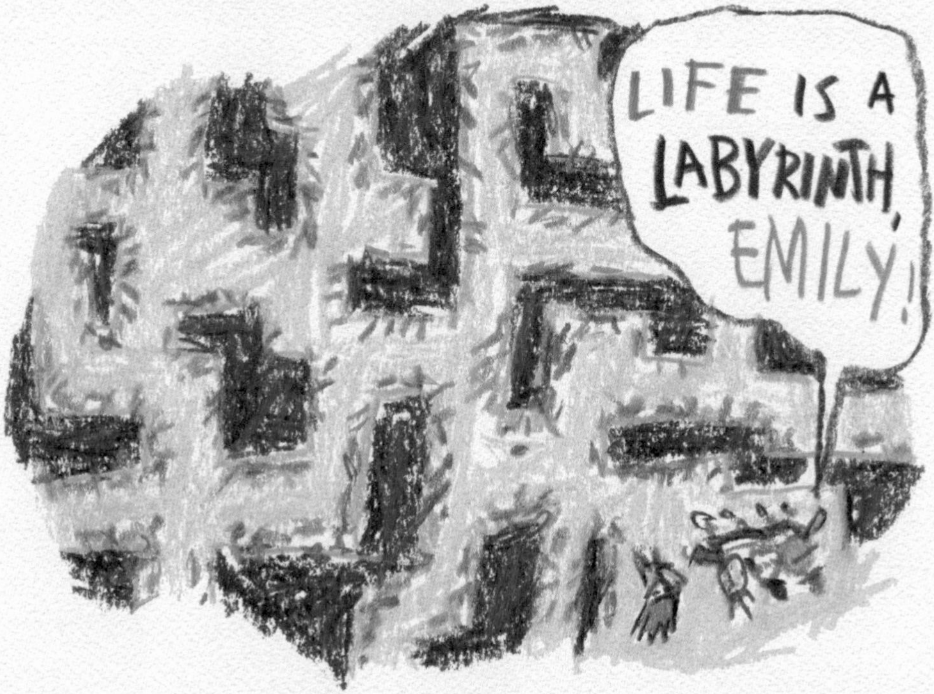
LIFE IS A LABYRINTH, EMILY!

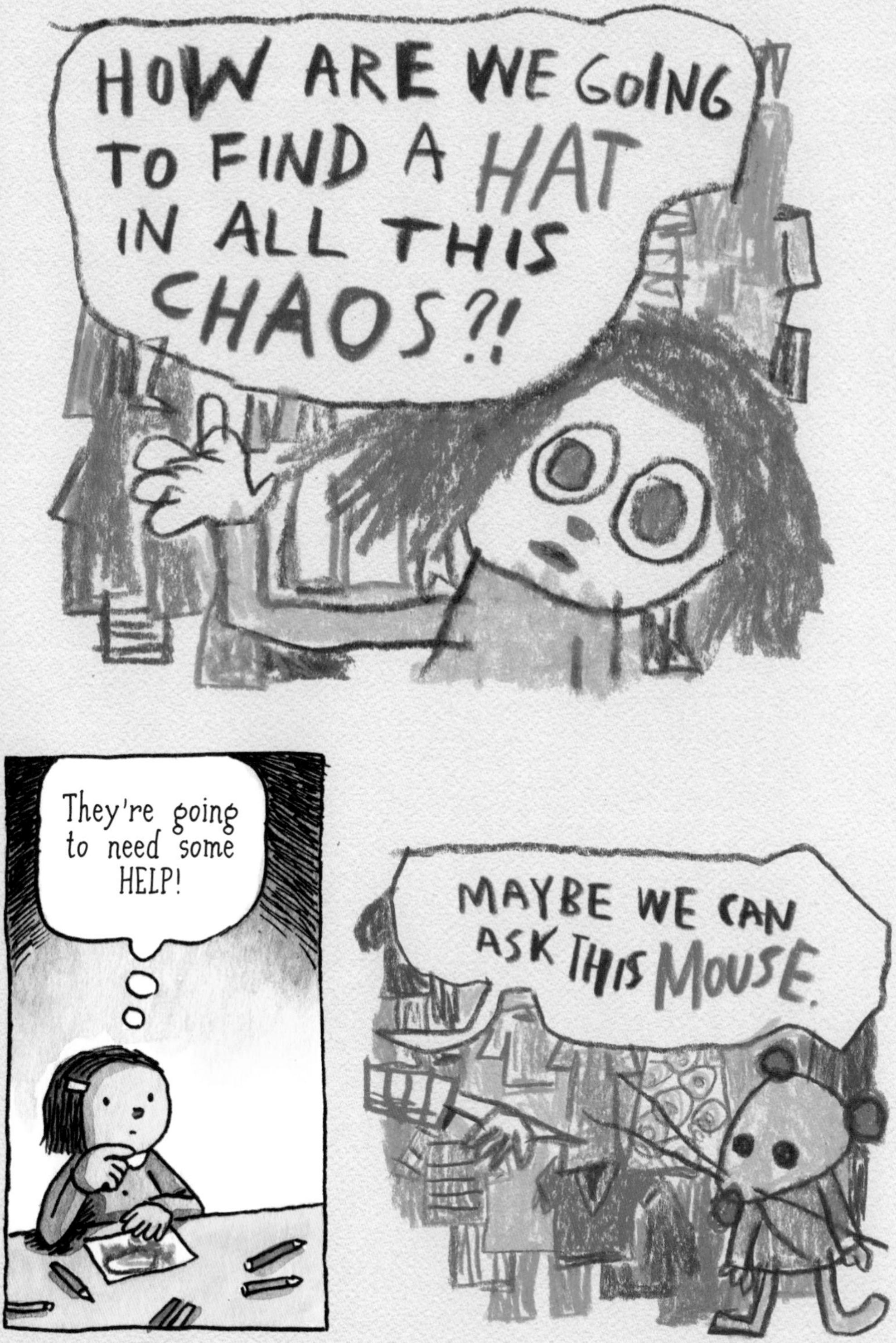
HOW ARE WE GOING TO FIND A HAT IN ALL THIS CHAOS?!
They're going to need some HELP!
MAYBE WE CAN ASK THIS MOUSE.

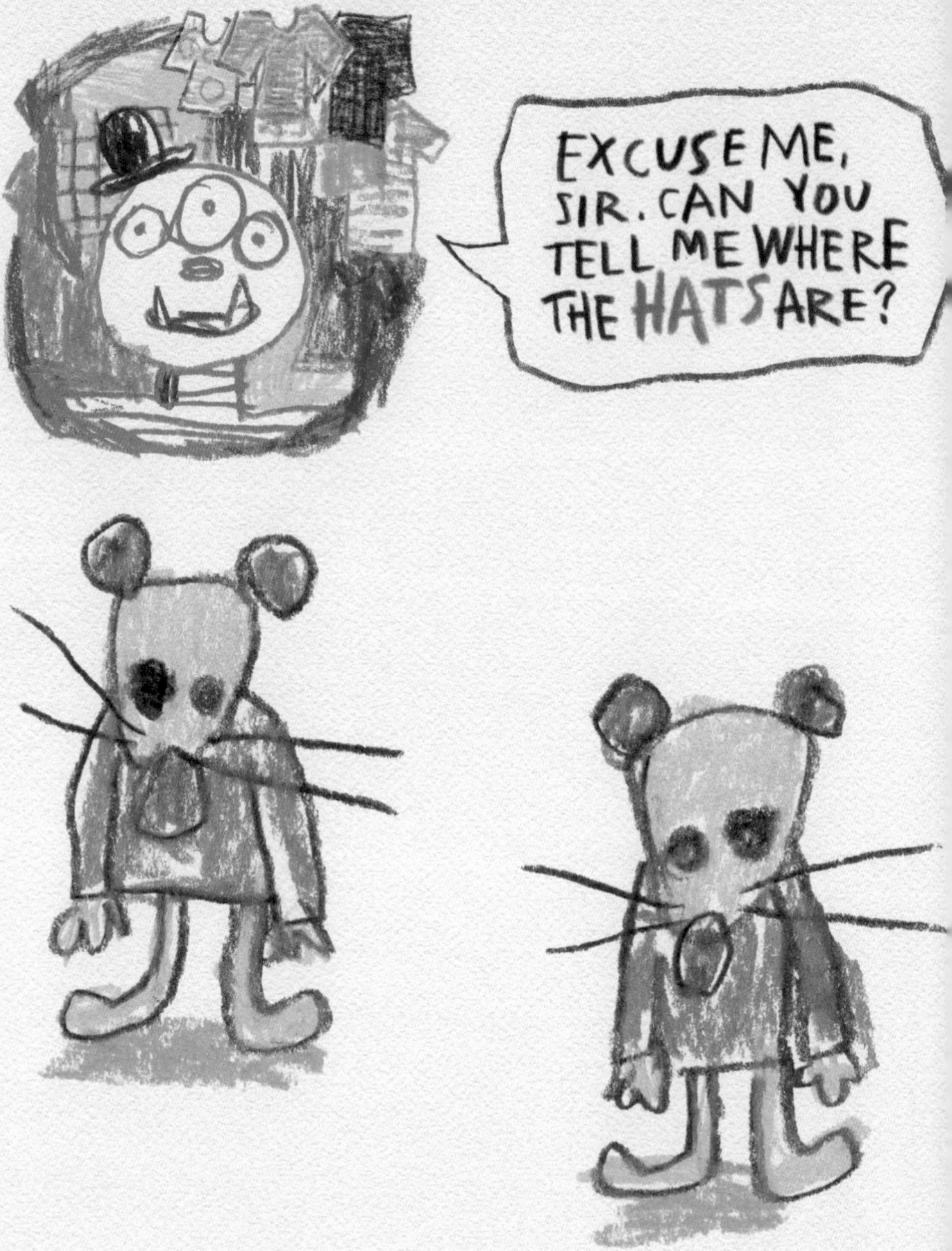
EXCUSE ME, SIR. CAN YOU TELL ME WHERE THE HATS ARE?

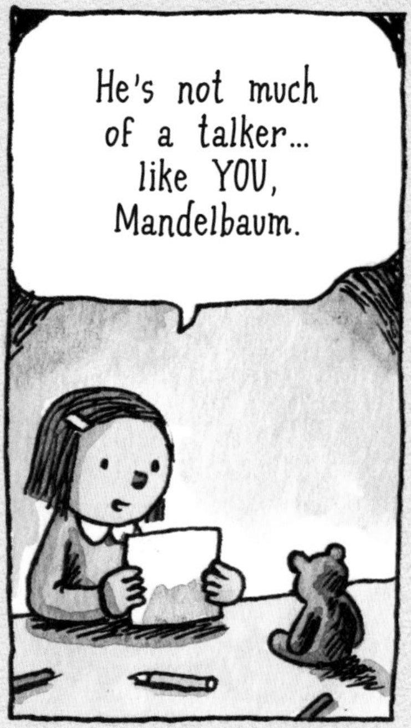
He's not much of a talker... like YOU, Mandelbaum.

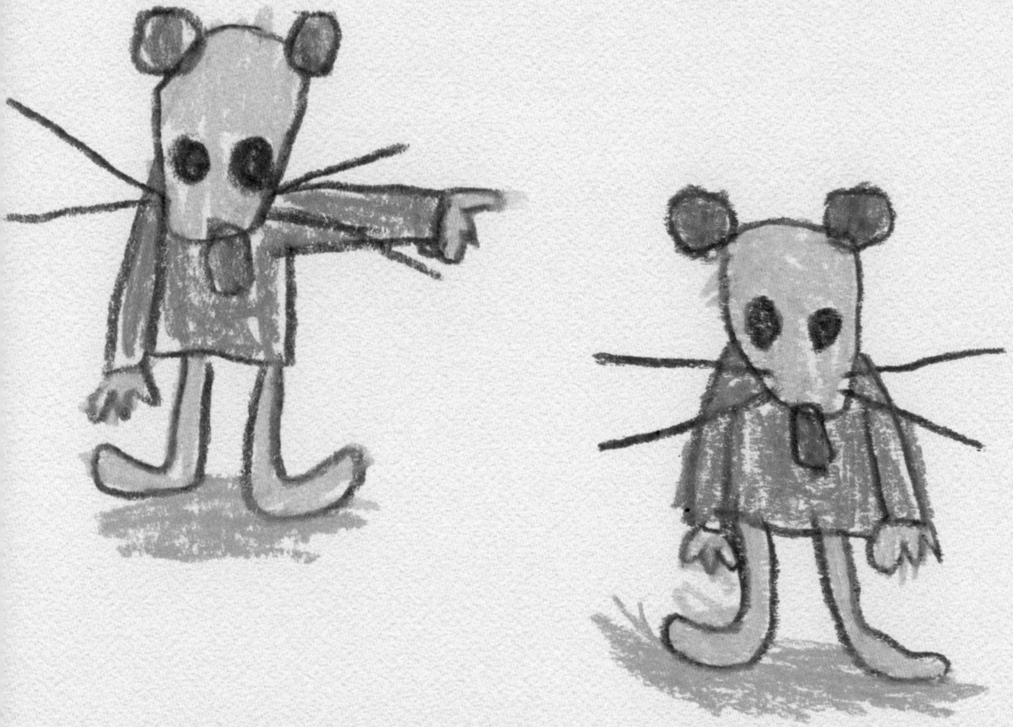

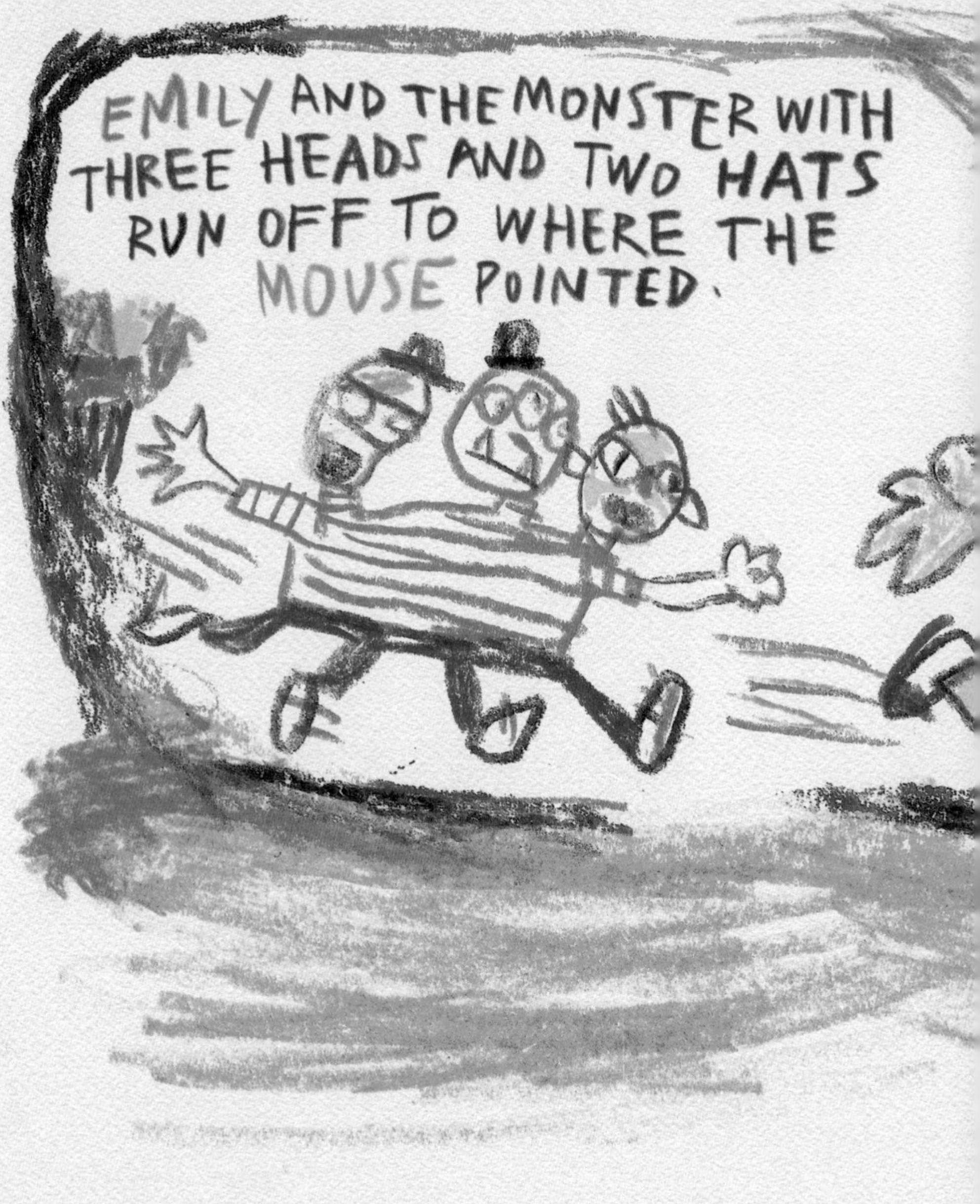
EMILY AND THE MONSTER WITH THREE HEADS AND TWO HATS RUN OFF TO WHERE THE MOUSE POINTED.

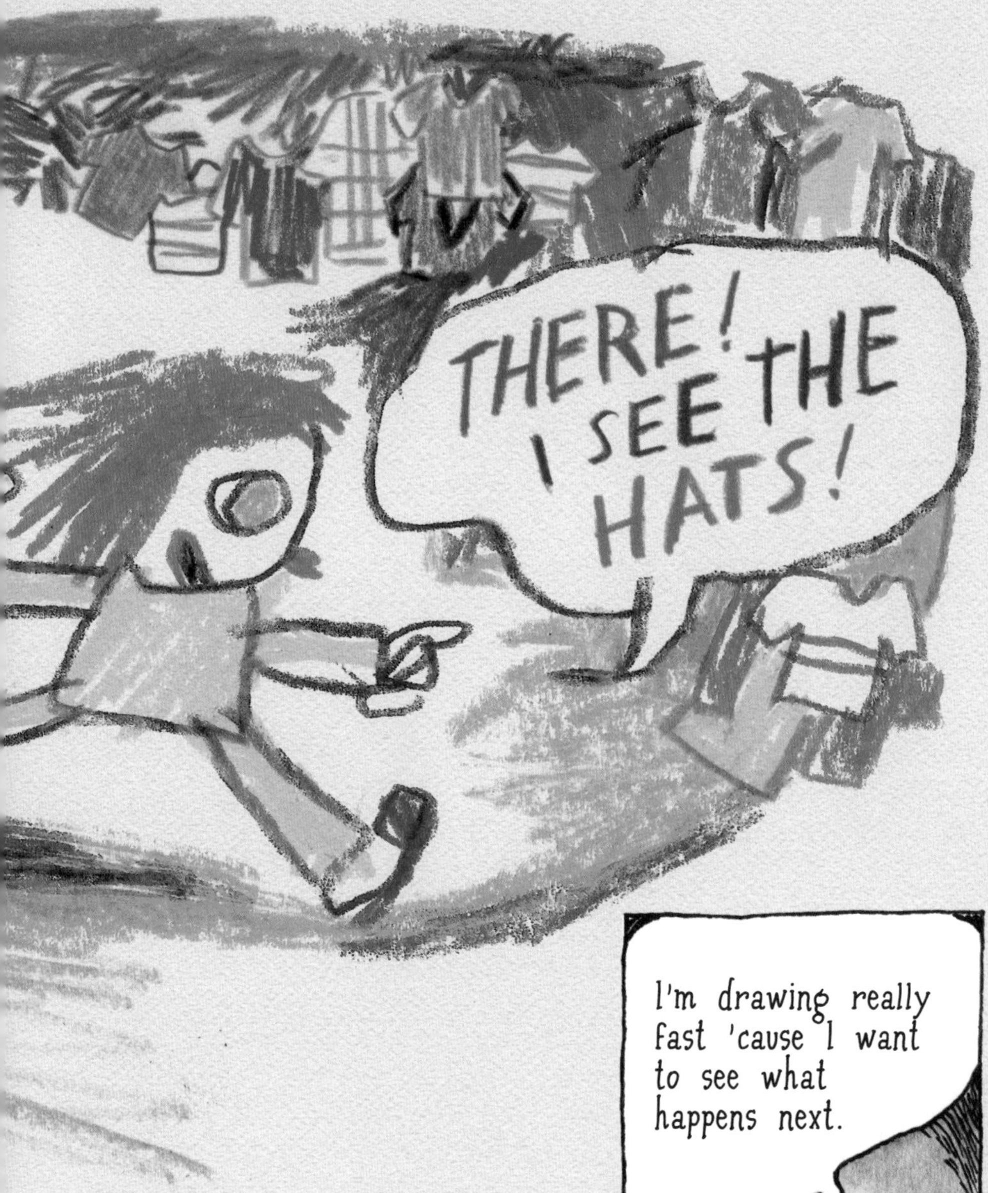
THERE! I SEE THE HATS!

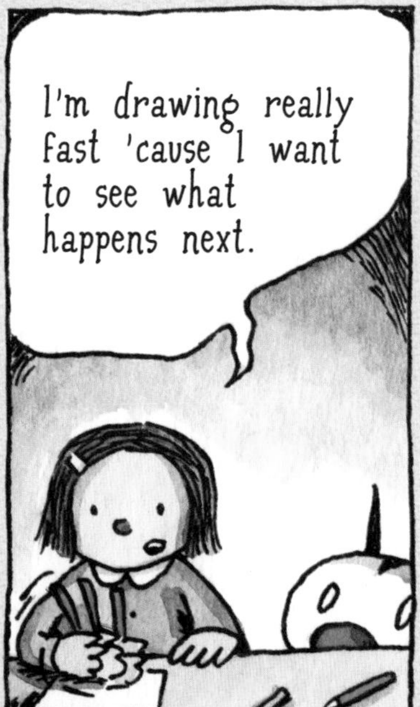
I'm drawing really fast 'cause I want to see what happens next.

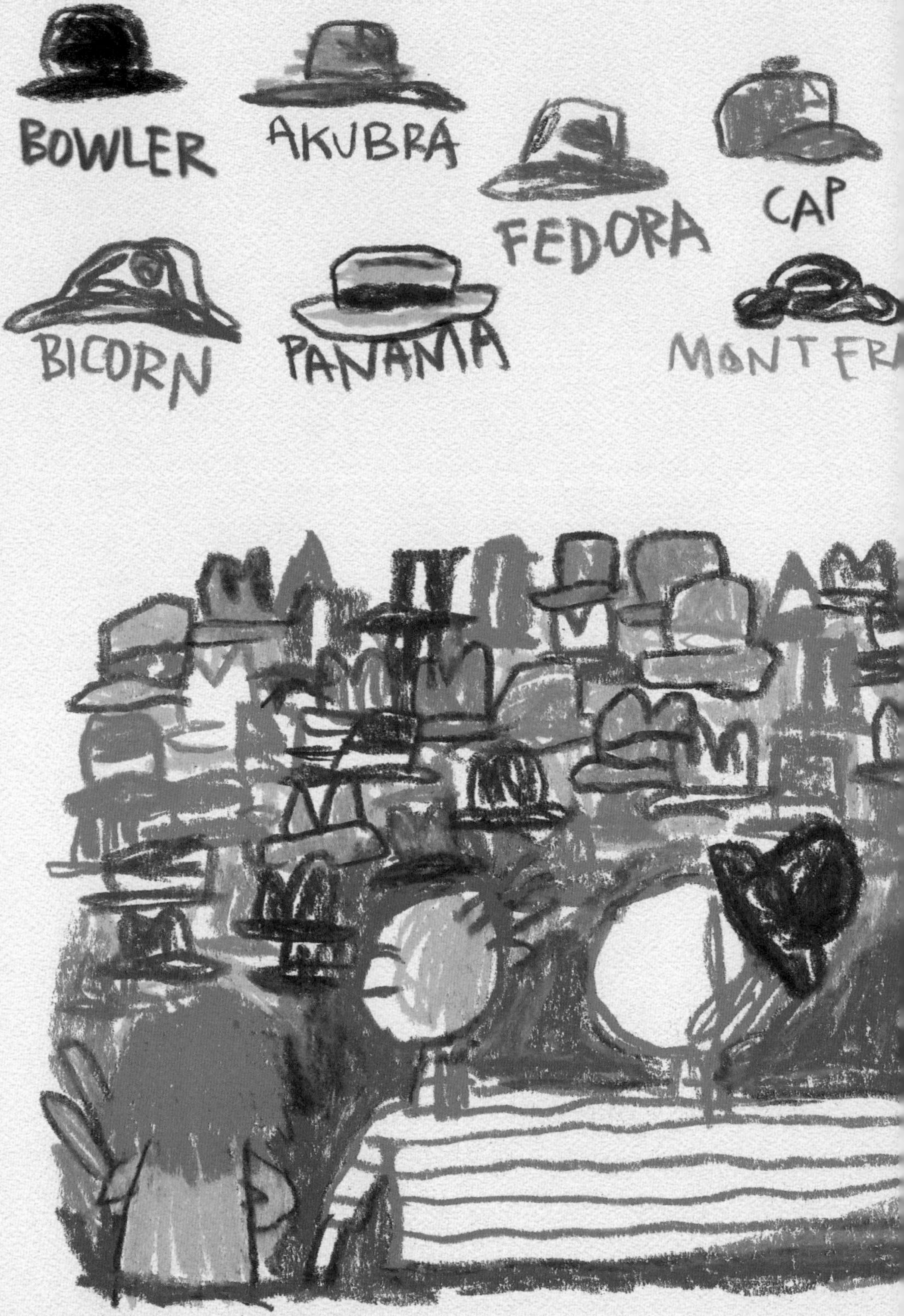
BOWLER
AKUBRA
FEDORA
CAP
BICORN
PANAMA
MONTER

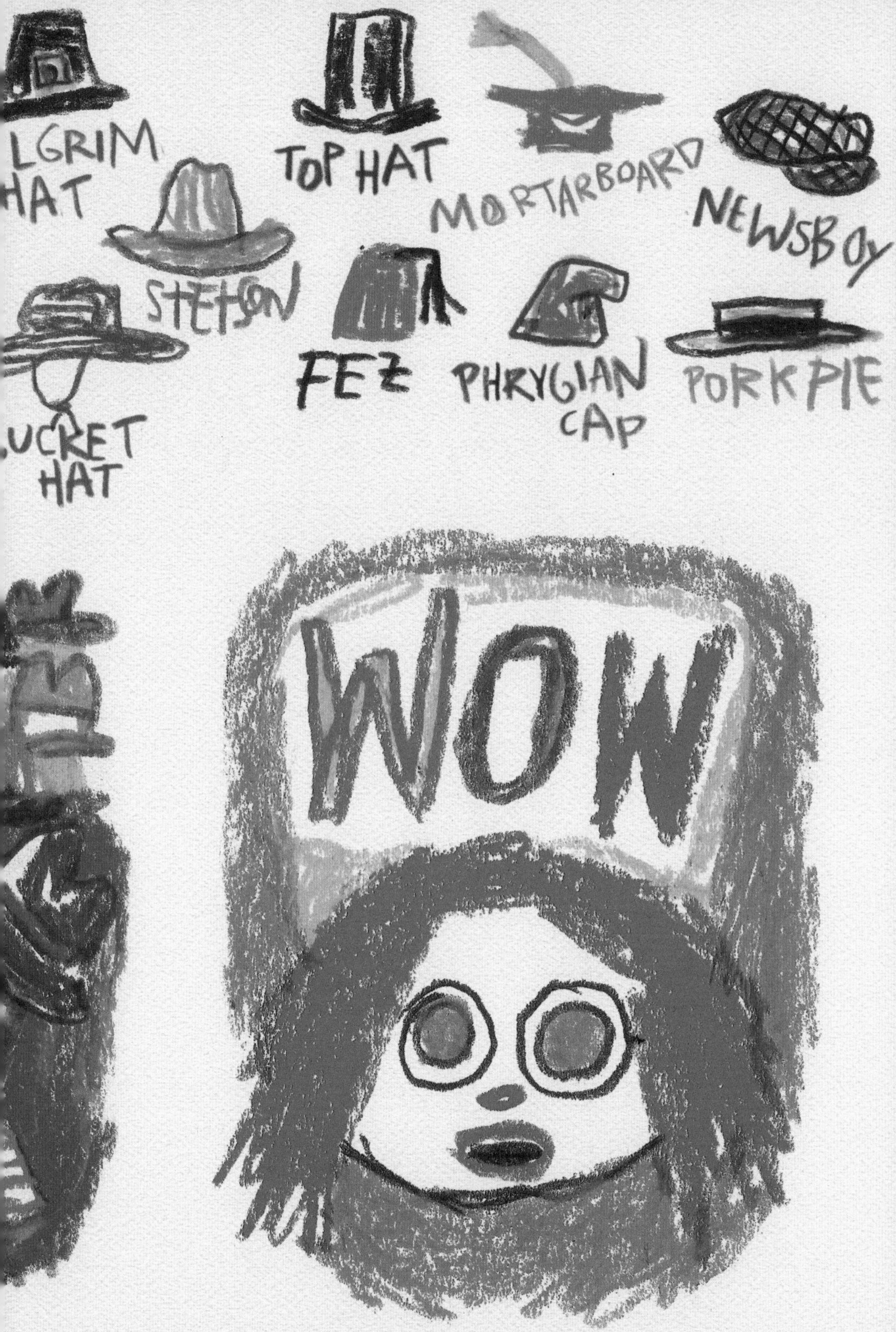
LGRIM HAT
TOP HAT
MORTARBOARD
NEWSBOY
STETSON
FEZ
PHRYGIAN CAP
PORKPIE
UCKET HAT
WOW

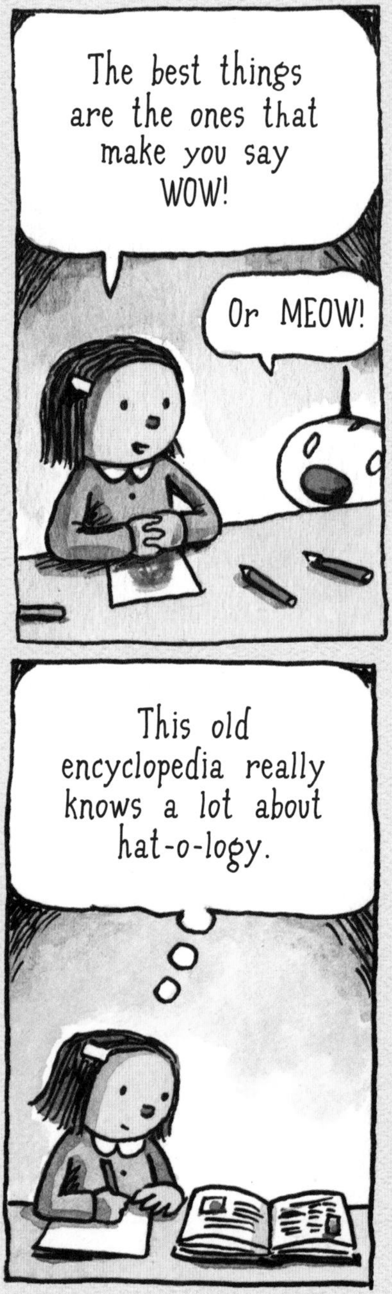
The best things are the ones that make you say WOW!
Or MEOW!
This old encyclopedia really knows a lot about hat-o-logy.

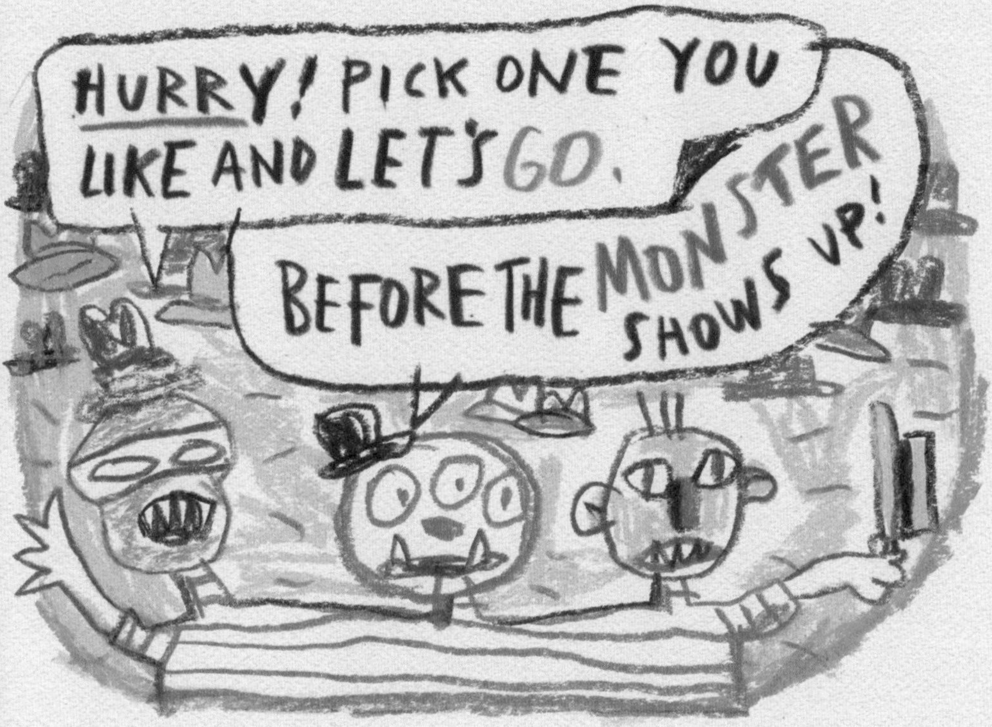
HURRY! PICK ONE YOU LIKE AND LET'S GO.
BEFORE THE MONSTER SHOWS UP!

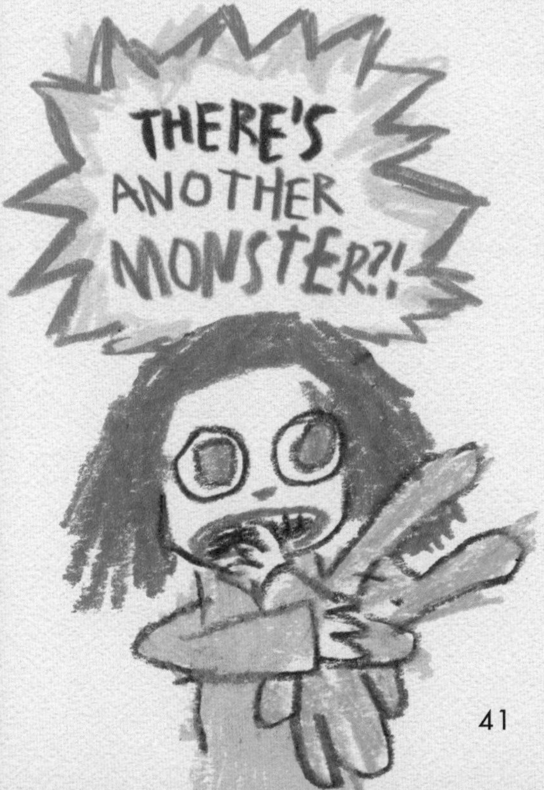
THERE'S ANOTHER MONSTER?!

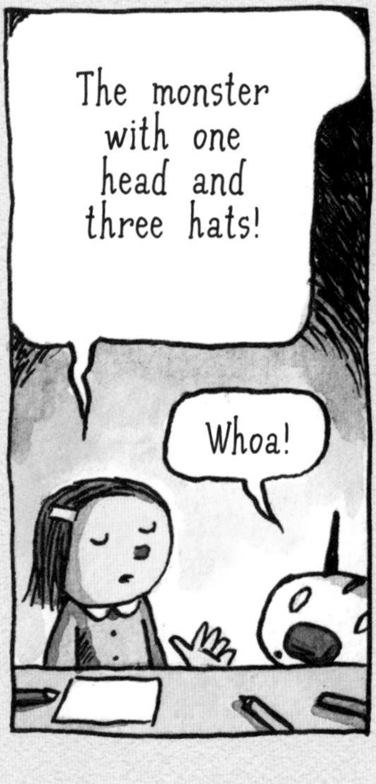
The monster with one head and three hats!
Whoa!

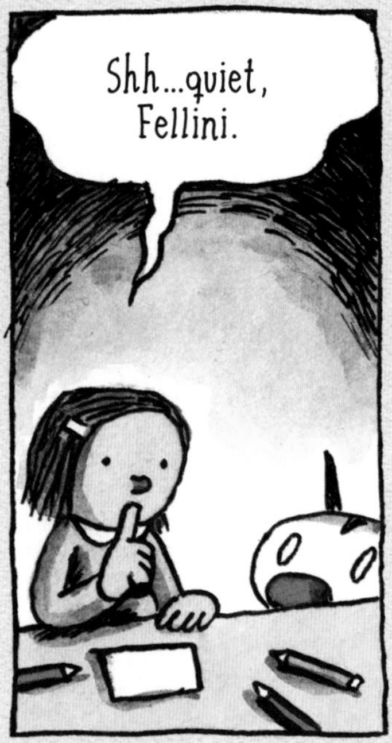
Shh...quiet, Fellini.

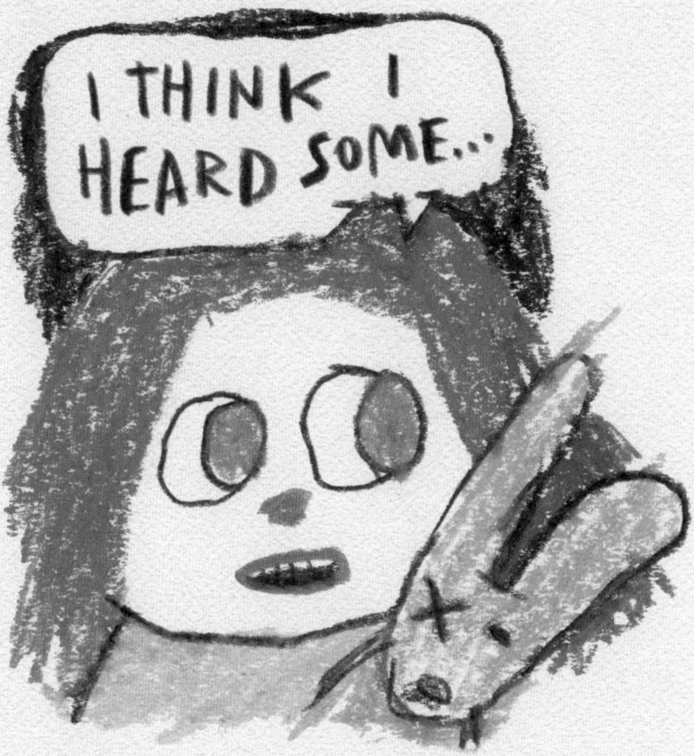
I THINK I HEARD SOME...

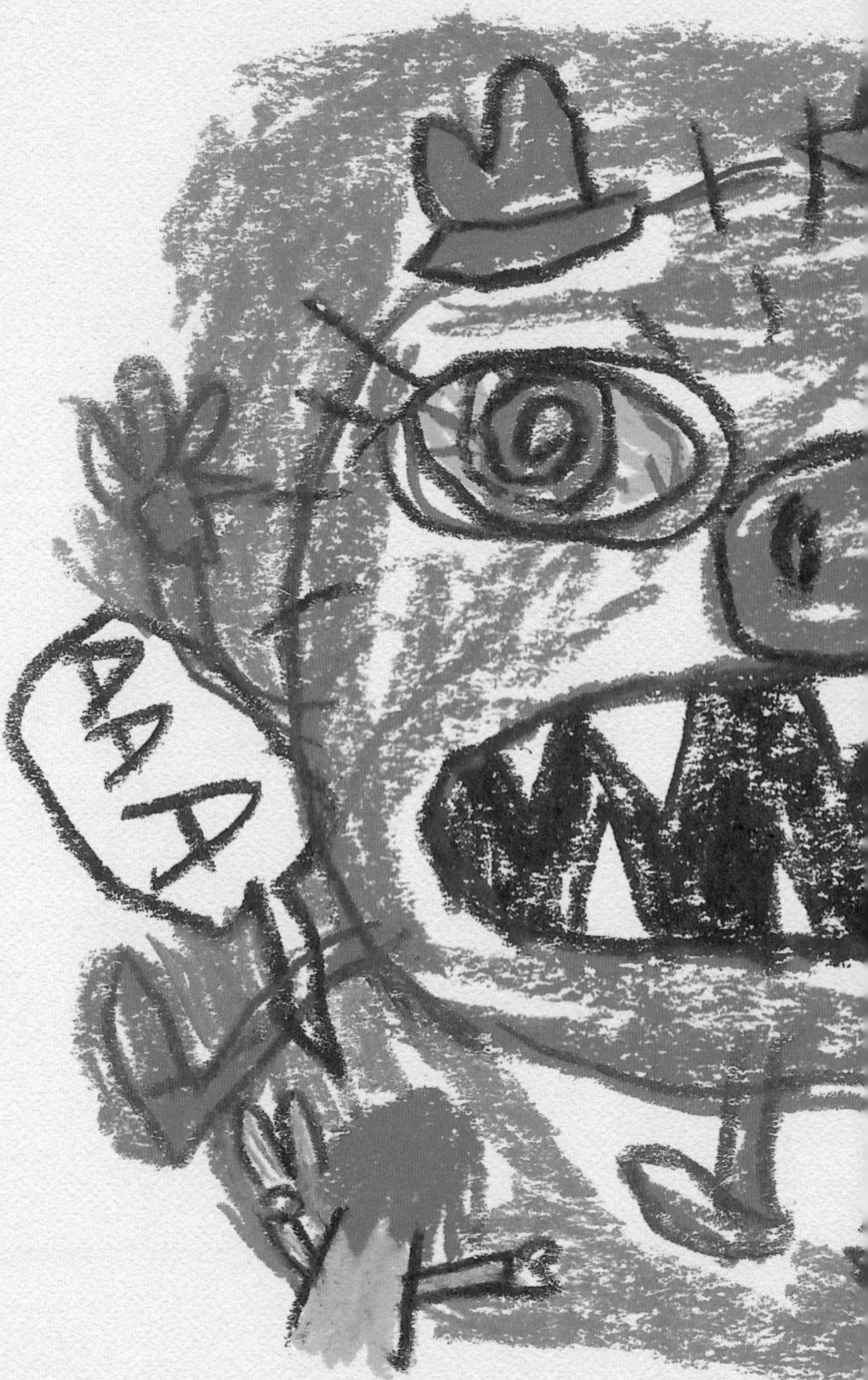
AAA

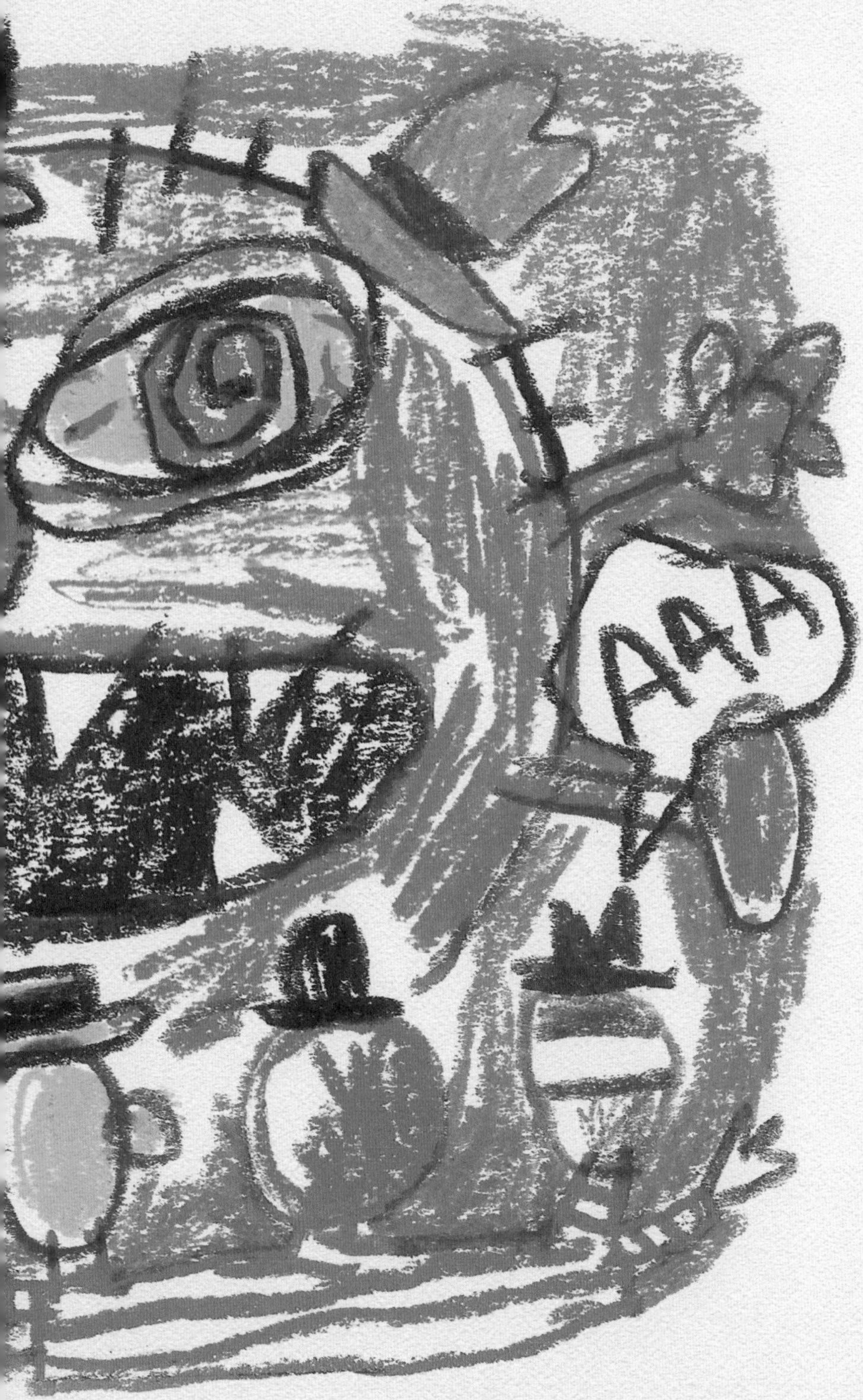
AAA

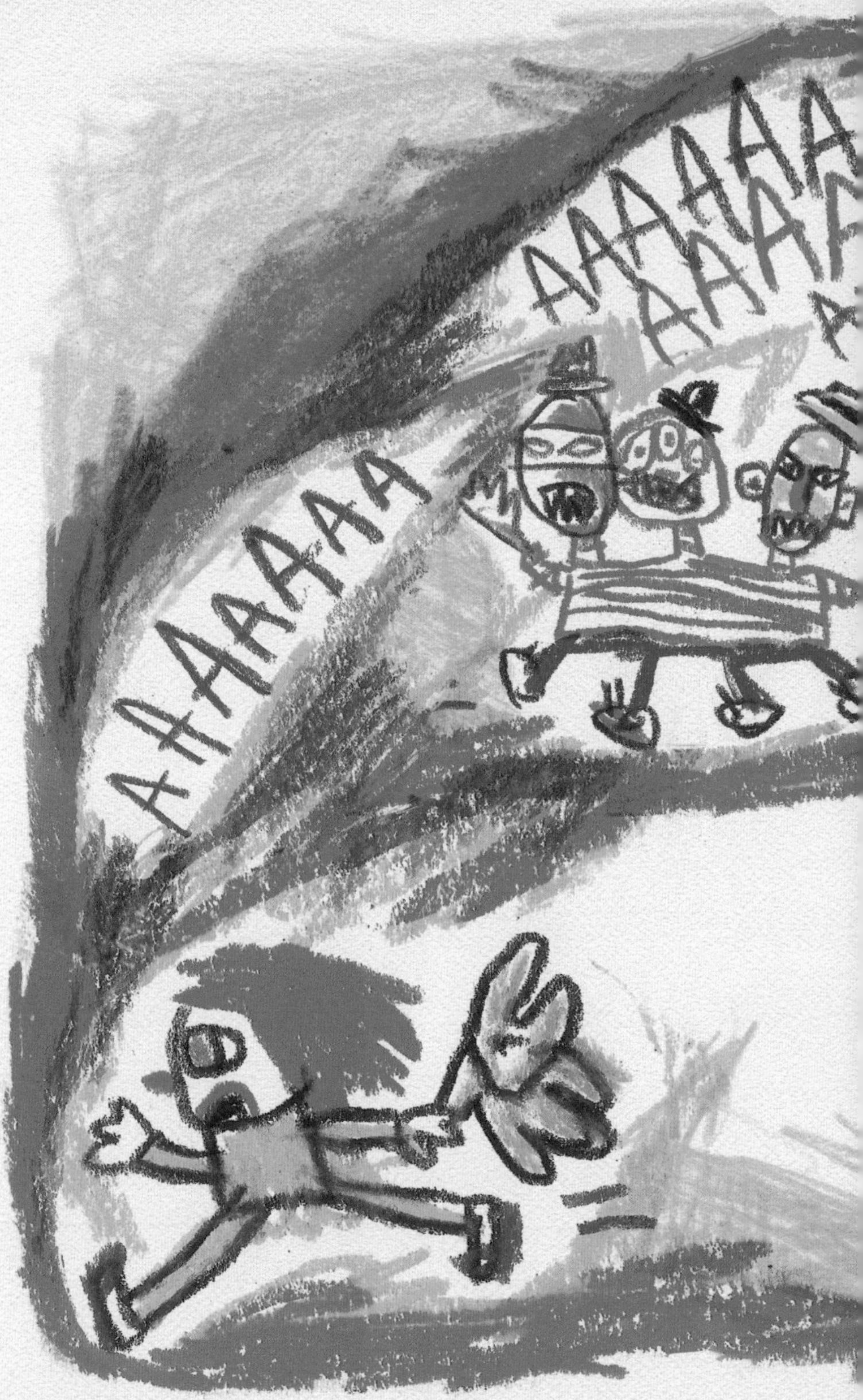
AAAAAAAAAAAA

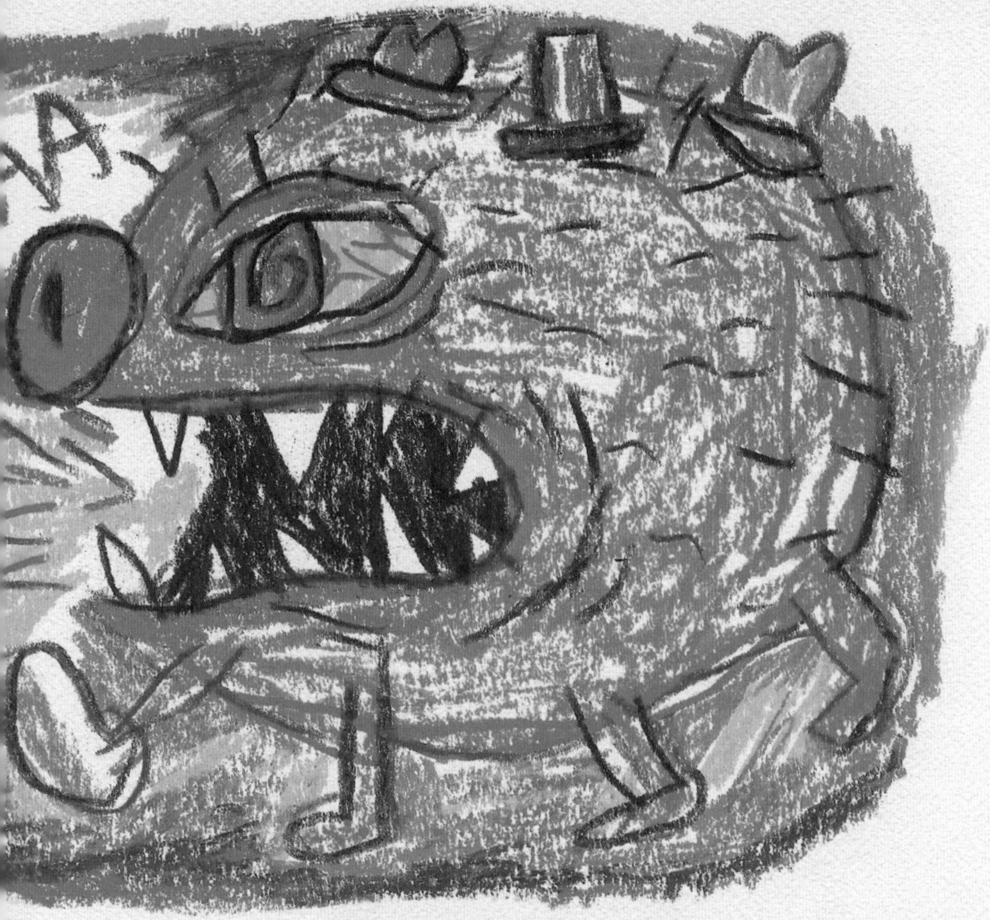

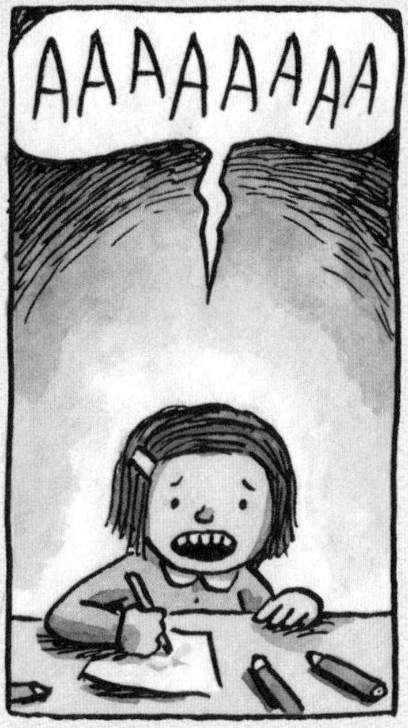
AAAAAAAA

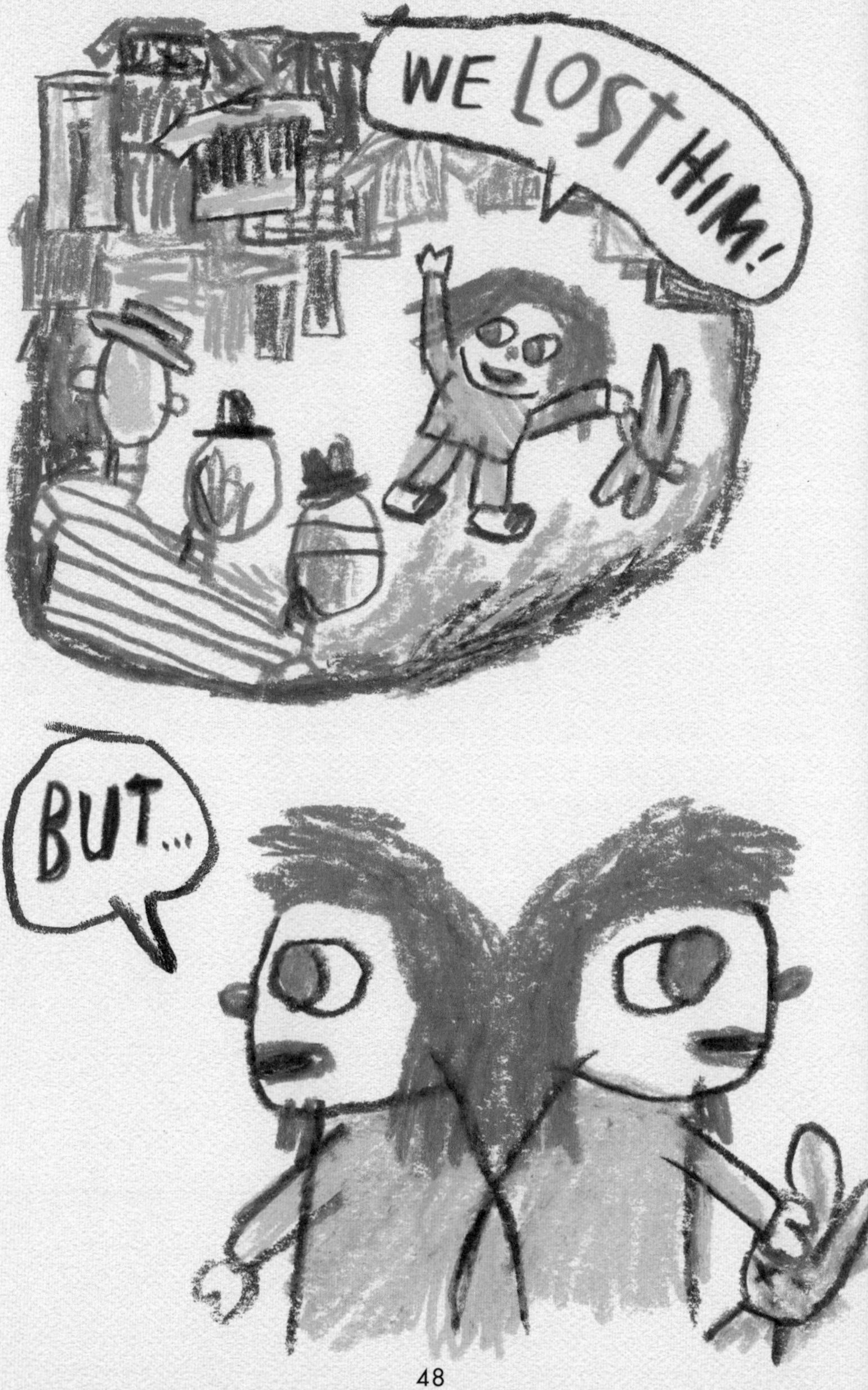
WE LOST HIM!
BUT...

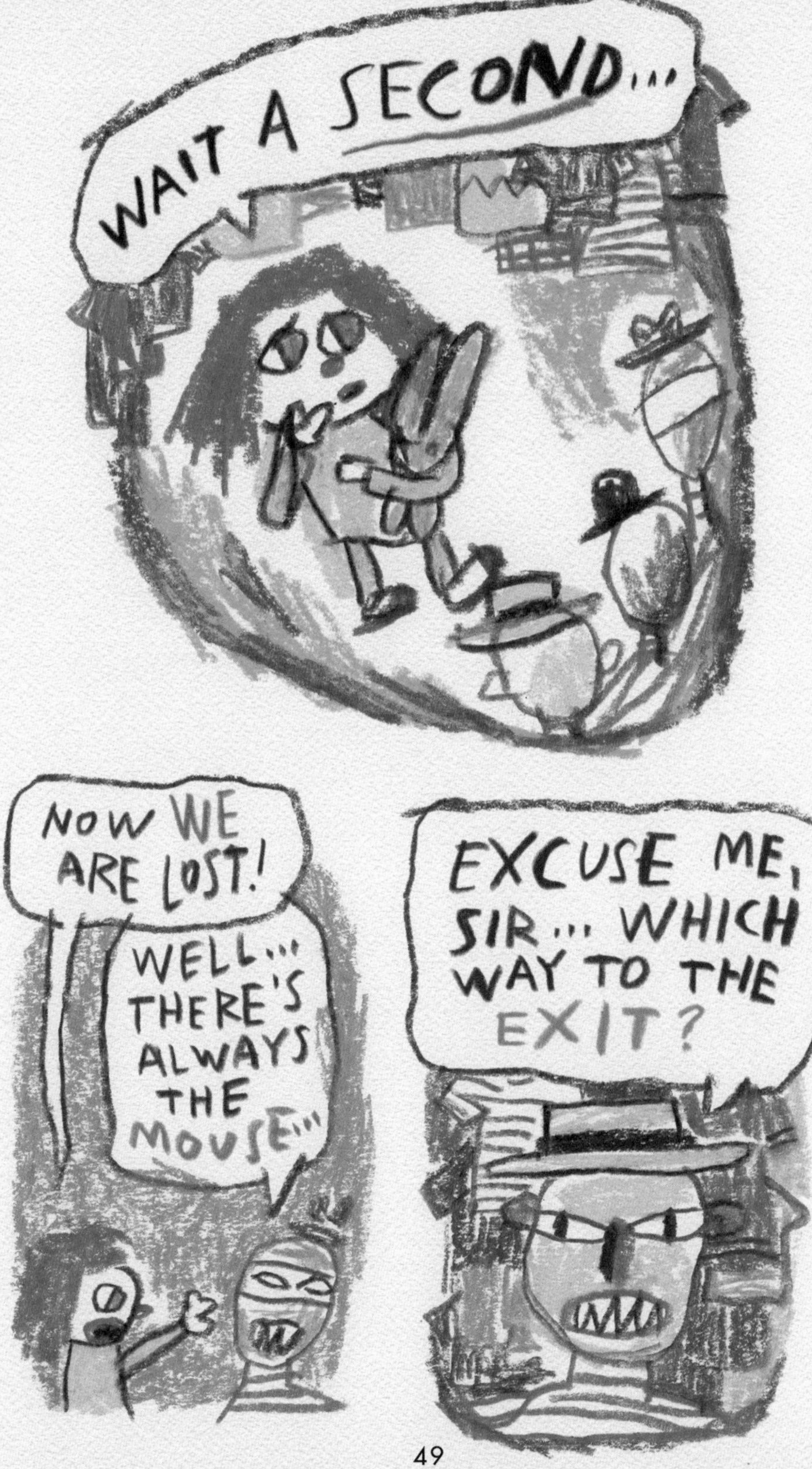
WAIT A SECOND...
NOW WE ARE LOST!
WELL... THERE'S ALWAYS THE MOUSE...
EXCUSE ME, SIR... WHICH WAY TO THE EXIT?

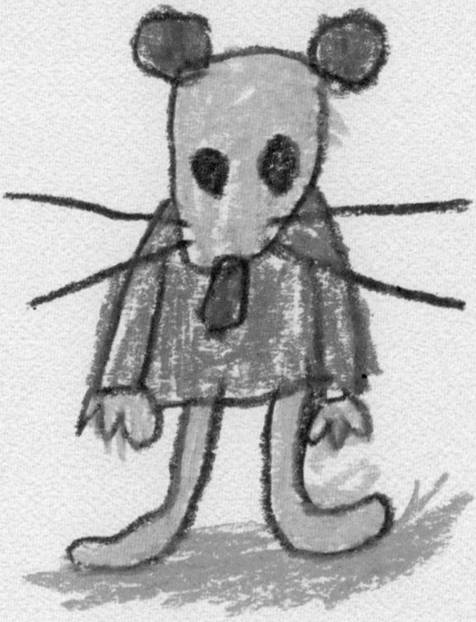

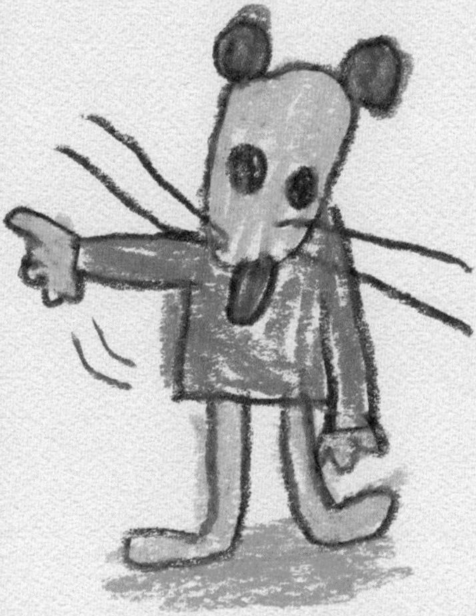

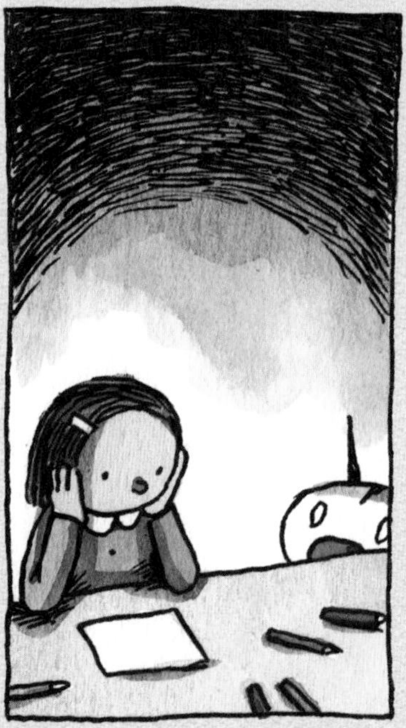

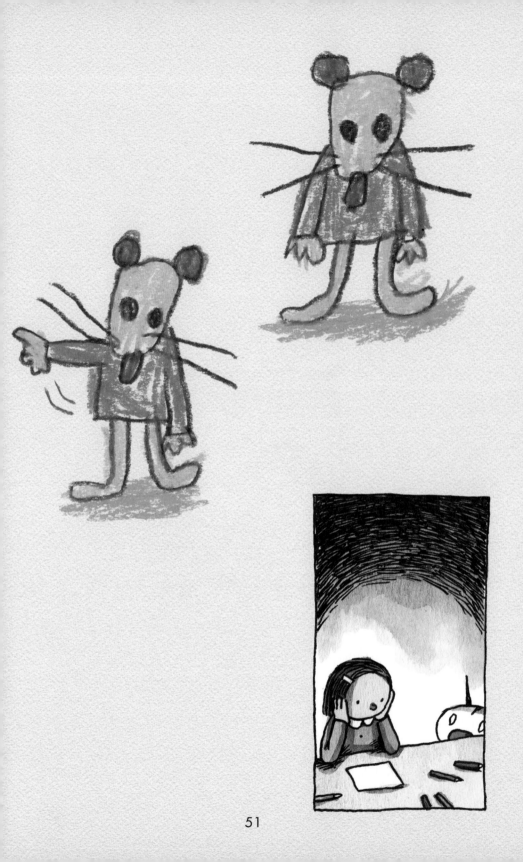

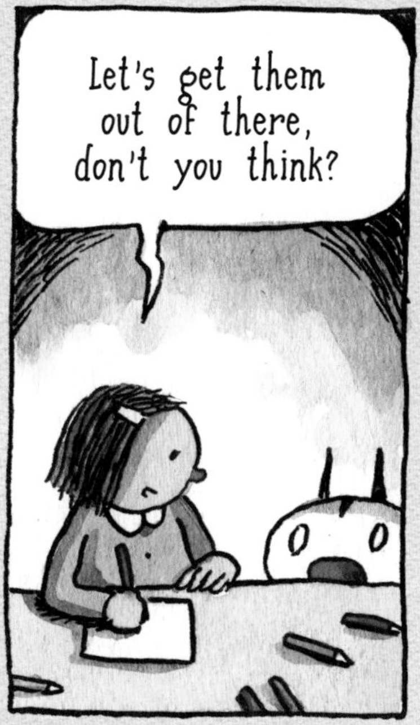
Let's get them out of there, don't you think?

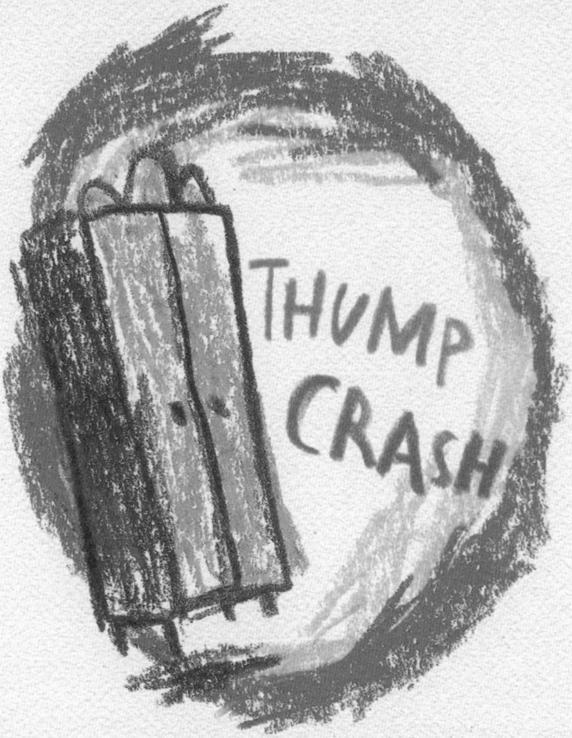
THUMP
CRASH

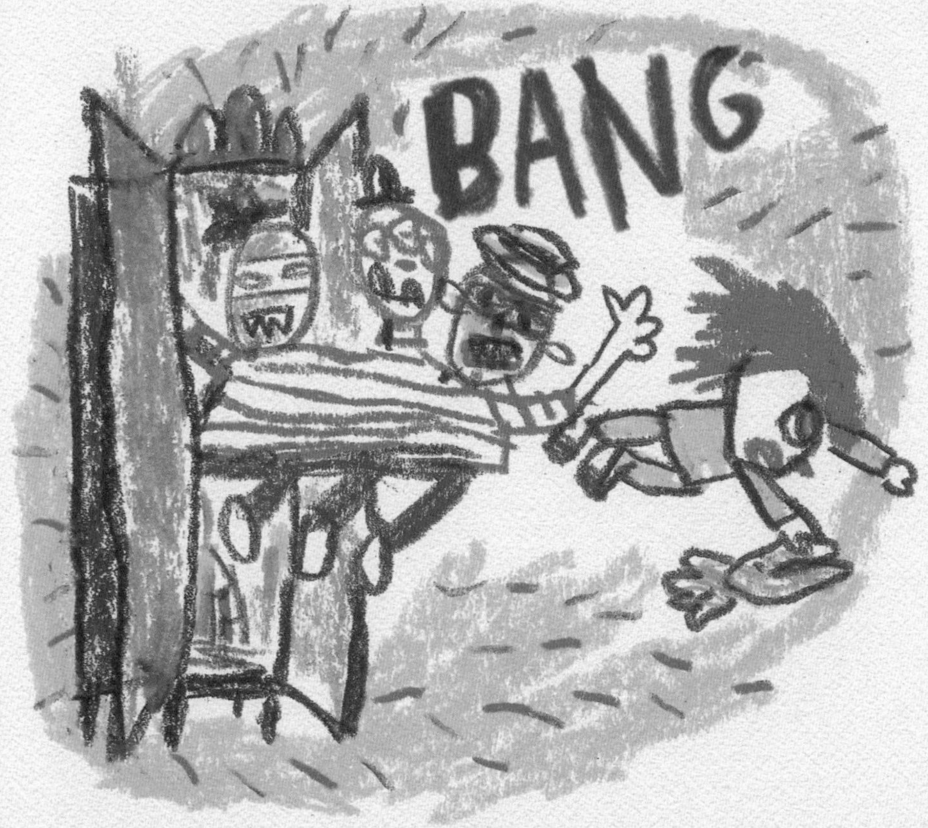
BANG

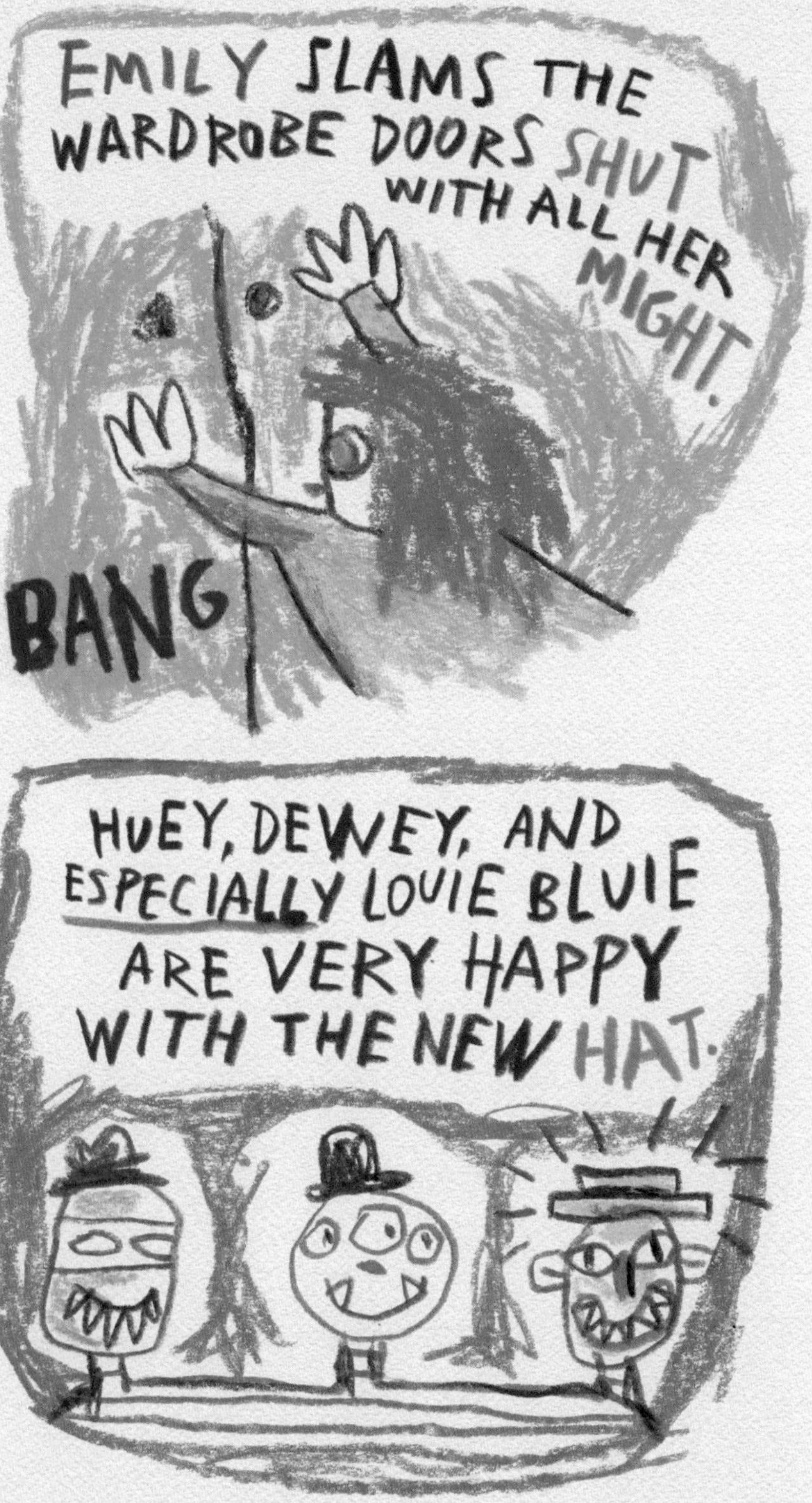
EMILY SLAMS THE WARDROBE DOORS SHUT WITH ALL HER MIGHT.
BANG
HUEY, DEWEY, AND ESPECIALLY LOUIE BLUIE ARE VERY HAPPY WITH THE NEW HAT.

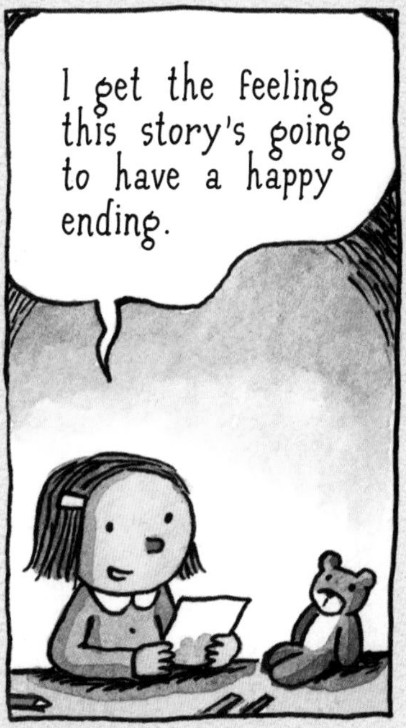
I get the feeling this story's going to have a happy ending.

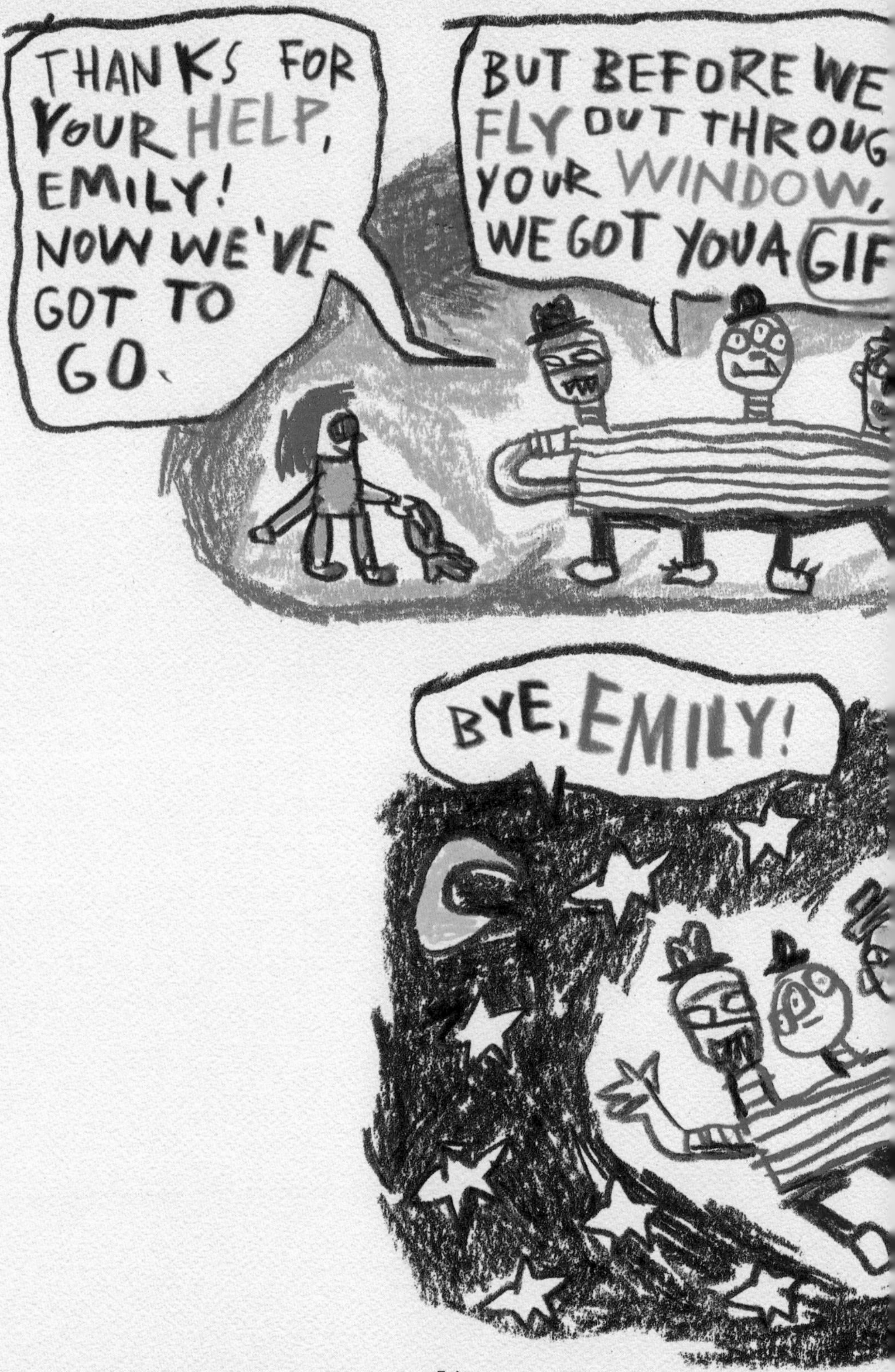
THANKS FOR YOUR HELP, EMILY! NOW WE'VE GOT TO GO.
BUT BEFORE WE FLY OUT THROUG YOUR WINDOW, WE GOT YOU A GIF
BYE, EMILY!

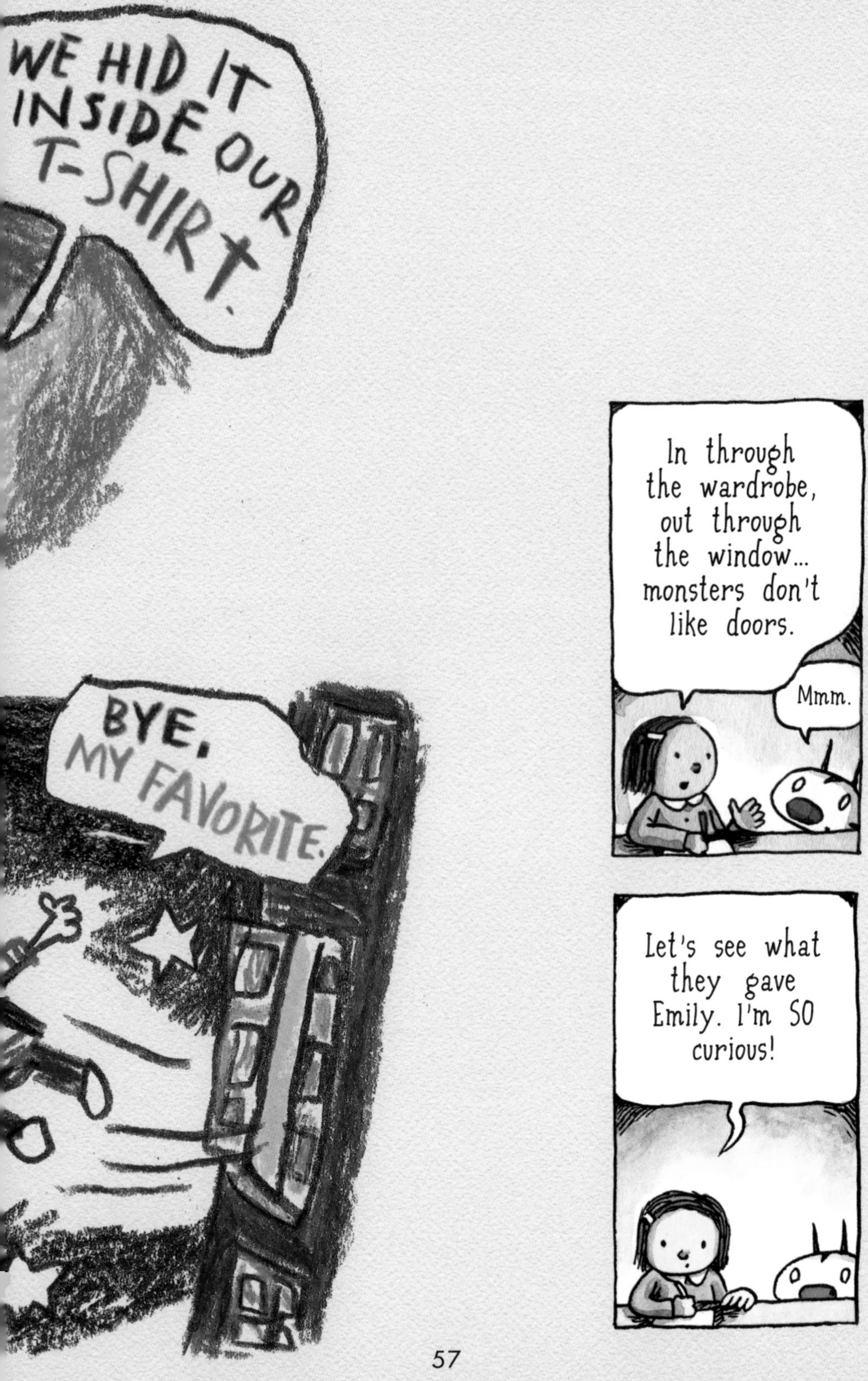
WE HID IT INSIDE OUR T-SHIRT.
BYE, MY FAVORITE.
In through the wardrobe, out through the window... monsters don't like doors.
Mmm.
Let's see what they gave Emily. I'm SO curious!

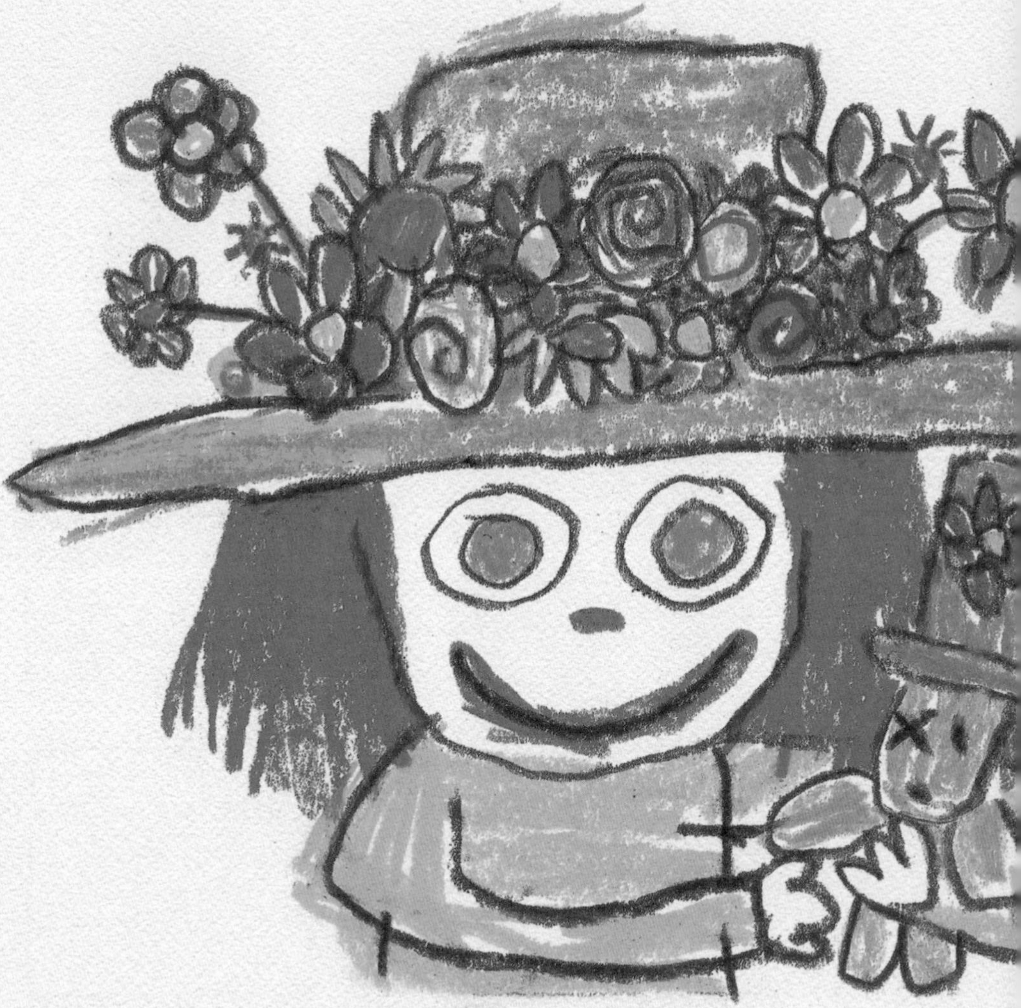

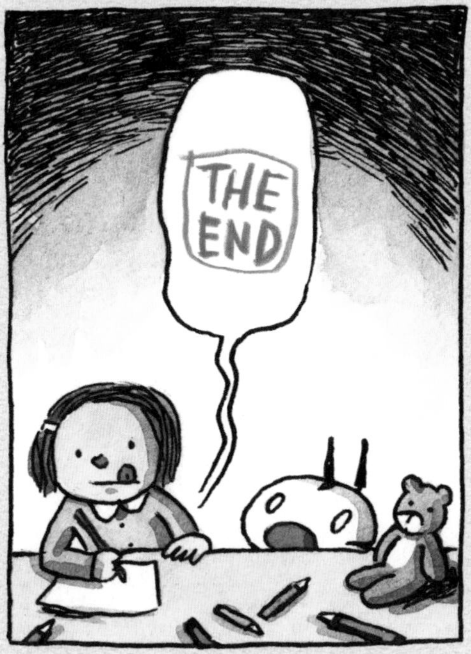
THE END

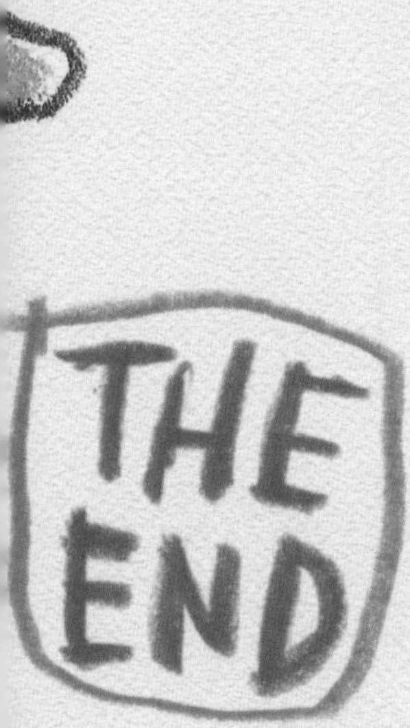
THE END

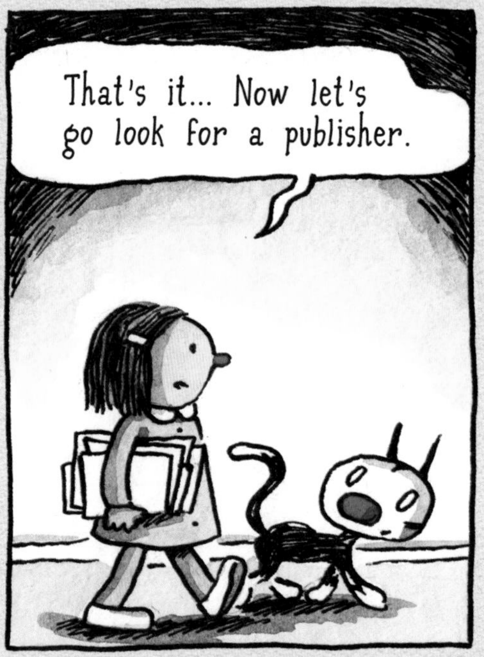
That's it... Now let's go look for a publisher.

ABOUT THE AUTHOR

RICARDO SIRI LINIERS, known as LINIERS, is the author of *Macanudo*, a daily comic strip hugely popular in Argentina, now available in English. His U.S. debut, *The Big Wet Balloon*, a TOON Book, was nominated for an Eisner Award and chosen as one of *Parents'* Top 10 Children's Books. He lives in Buenos Aires with his wife and three daughters, Matilda, Clementina, and Emma, whom he credits as the inspiration for this book.

HOW TO READ
COMICS WITH KIDS

Kids **love** comics! They are naturally drawn to the details in the pictures, which make them want to read the words. Comics beg for repeated readings and let both emerging and reluctant readers enjoy complex stories with a rich vocabulary. But since comics have their own grammar, here are a few tips for reading them with kids:

GUIDE YOUNG READERS Use your finger to show your place in the text, but keep it at the bottom of the speaking character so it doesn't hide the very important facial expressions.

HAM IT UP! Think of the comic book story as a play, and don't hesitate to read with expression and intonation. Assign parts or get kids to supply the sound effects, a great way to reinforce phonics skills.

LET THEM GUESS. Comics provide lots of context for the words so emerging readers can make informed guesses. Like jigsaw puzzles, comics ask readers to make connections, so check a young audience's understanding by asking, "What's this character thinking?" (But don't be surprised if a kid finds some of the comics' subtle details faster than you).

TALK ABOUT THE PICTURES. Point out how the artist paces the story with pauses (silent panels) or speeded-up action (a burst of short panels). Discuss how the size and shape of the panels carry meaning.

ABOVE ALL, ENJOY! There is of course never one right way to read, so go for the shared pleasure. Once children make the story happen in their imagination, they have discovered the thrill of reading, and you won't be able to stop them. At that point, just go get them more books, and more comics.

www.TOON-BOOKS.com

SEE OUR FREE ONLINE CARTOON MAKERS, LESSON PLANS, AND MUCH MORE.